Houses of the Broken

Katherine Alton

This is a work of fiction. Names, characters, places, and incidents either are the product of the author's imagination or are used fictitiously. Any resemblance to actual persons, living or dead, events, or locales is entirely coincidental.

ISBN: 0989583805
ISBN-13: 978-0-9895838-0-0

First Paperback Edition

To my dear husband, Johnny.
Thank you for giving me the time.

ACKNOWLEDGMENTS

A special thank-you to my brilliant photographer Shane Montross for providing healthy peer pressure and inspiring illustrations for the story.
To Marie for keeping the evil genius on track.
To my parents for not turning me in…
To Matt and Larry for providing constructive criticism.
Many thanks to all my friends who were willing to read and re-read at a moment's notice.
And again, thank you to my husband Johnny, for the love and support he provided in this endeavor.

-1-

I have the darkness; it breathes inside me.

Twenty years since I left that place and it's still not been long enough. I swore I'd never go back but time passes, memories fade, and the gnawing longing for the familiar tugs at you.

I would like to say it was a dark and stormy night, fraught with peril when I peeled out of the driveway, but it wasn't. It was a Tuesday, partly cloudy, unseasonably warm, and traffic was surprisingly light. The weight of my decision seemed somehow swept away by the smell of unused air conditioning lazily puffing a winters' worth of dust and debris through my vents. My hair swirled slightly in the breeze as the sound of Tom Petty's voice droned out of the local classic rock station. To this day I'm convinced one of his songs can be found on a station anywhere, at any time of day. But it's only a theory.

A look in the rear view mirror. Trying to surmise more than just the traffic patterns and the possible speed trap I just blew through. A heavy squint reveals no more

1

answers than I already have. *Glance away before you see the sigh escape through your lightly parted lips.* This was the game I played with myself down the miles of broken roads I knew better than to travel.

Would she be gray? Frail? Old? Would the light have left her eyes? Would she even know us, even care?

It was my own damn fault for answering the phone call. In a world of caller ID, I had no excuse. This is what happens when you're not paying attention. Let your guard down and pay the price.

"Sis? DON'T HANG UP!..." Silence from my end of the line. *"It's mom..."* Shit.

A pain shoots through my temple just thinking about it. I cast my eyes around the car to give them a chance to refocus. I swear my odometer mocks me as it happily trips the 106,666 mile mark. Sometimes the Universe thinks it's funny.

I don't want to be there. I don't want to go there. It's better if I'm not. It's better for everyone involved.

The car gave a reluctant chug as I hit the state line. This old land yacht wasn't fit for distance any more, but it would have to do. For that matter, neither was I. A pit stop for us both sounded like a good idea to take the edge off. It was about time to top off my fluids anyhow.

A gas station and a small motel with a lounge appeared and I was in heaven. I grabbed my notebook and map, then pulled my hat down over my eyes. I wasn't looking for conversation, but it had a way of finding me, no matter how I seemed to master the art of looking unapproachable. People get bored. People get curious. People liked to strike up bets with their buddies. In short, people like to stick their nose where it doesn't belong.

A nice seat in the far dark end of the bar was fine. Someone gets close, and a simple swivel towards the wall is as effective as bricks and mortar. Usually.

The evening was still young so the usual crew hadn't quite settled in yet. There were a few, clearly of local color, that smelled of unemployment, carefully guarding their piles of empty bottles. Pickling was their last real shot at living to a ripe old age.

The bar tender sidled up with a 'hon' and a smile

that bore the brunt of too much nicotine and hard times. No doubt her days of glory were spent making time in the back seats of classic muscle cars that any red blooded baby boomer would give their capped and whitened eye teeth for these days.

My flicker of acknowledgment, for one of whatever was on special, and she was on her way. She was smart enough to read the body language, and for that I was grateful. She returned her attention to the regulars, whose Social Security checks no doubt kept her well supplied with the blue eye shadow that was her trademark. People had to make a living. Who was I to judge?

I nursed my watery excuse for a beer and studied my map. Turns out I had finally forgotten my way home. Living half way across the country helped dissipate the internal geographic markers. Tracing the routes with my finger, it started coming back... landmarks, rest stops, scenic overlooks. The interstate, while quicker, had much less character to it. And while I was traveling on borrowed time, I didn't intend to break any land speed records. Nor could I if I even wanted to; ol' Bessie had seen better days. If I wasn't careful, I'd be figuring out the disposal of more than one lifeless shell by the end of this trip.

A sticky puff of unconditioned air caressing my cheek made me suddenly aware that the door of the place had been opening and closing with increasing frequency. I glanced at my watch. *Shit, happy hour.* I sunk down a little lower in my seat, nose nearly to the bar. Another frosty mug of piss water appeared before me before I could object. It was hard to protest an errant dollar draft. Plus it looked like it was the last one I would get until the wave of the great unwashed masses subsided.

I was wrong. Despite nursing and sipping the weak watered beverage in front of me, to the point of being bath water warm, finishing it immediately generated another in its place. This time I protested. "Oh I didn't wan--"

"Don't worry hon; it's from the gentlemen at the end of the bar."

I looked up long enough to see some freshly scrubbed dirt farmer tipping their finest John Deere hat. *Sigh*. What about my appearance and slouch wasn't screaming "Piss off"? Oh, right. The boobs. There was no jacket bulky enough to truly conceal the feminine figure, no matter how slight. -- Especially in a one-horse bar like this. Fresh meat was fresh meat. Couldn't blame a boy for wanting to put a fork in his family tree, right?

The increasingly agitated movements in my peripheral vision warned me that it wouldn't be long before a little more liquid courage brought some stranger tapping at my chamber door. The scent of prey was on the wind.

Cue Bachelor Number One. I really wasn't in the mood to play the dating game. Take it away, Chuck...

"You're not from around here, are you?"

Really? That was the best the brain trust could come up with? Plan number one... feign deafness.

Slightly louder, but still trying to be subtle, he seemed fairly sure the noise in the bar was to blame for the lack of response. "You're not from around here. Are you?"

My gaze doesn't break from the trail of condensation trickling down the edge of my once full mug.

"What gave it away, the fact that I wasn't at your family reunion?"

An uncomfortable snort, a slight readjustment and a quick glance to make sure the buddies didn't see Strike One go down in the record books. I felt the space to my right grow narrower.

"A sense of humor... Ain't nothing wrong with that. I mean, look how you're dressed."

Clearly the warning shot had gone unheeded.

"Listen, Jethro, no offense, but I'm not interested. If you're looking to recoup your share of the dollar draft, I'm sure I have thirty three cents here somewhere..."

"Oh, you think you're a god-damned comedian, dontcha? Someone clearly wasn't raised with the proper manners."

No, in fact, I wasn't. Go away Jethro, go away. *Finesse and misdirection, a noble choice but I'm just not in the mood tonight and the odds aren't in my favor anyhow. I should politely extricate myself from this situation but it's been a long day and I'm feeling punchy.*

"Tsk tsk tsk Jethro, that's no way to talk to a lady. We are the weak, the delicate, the timid mothers of life and nature."

"What you are MA'AM is a big city bitch."

Sigh. Why is that always the first response that big words evoke from little brains?

-3-

Two hours later and I'm back on the road, Bessie loaded down with unforeseen circumstances. She gives a belligerent chug as I blow through a set of washboard pot holes, nearly sending her less-than-polished hubcaps spinning off the road in various directions. I really needed to get those shocks looked at.

Eyes bleary, my fingers try to tune in the radio dial to something other than the country that makes my skin want to crawl. Naturally, next up... Tom Petty. I'm going to prove this hypothesis yet. Or at least the DJ's of middle America are going to do it for me.

Darkness surrounds, highlighted only by the vision of yellow lines in my headlights that hypnotize me as I wind my way through the back roads. I hear another chug and suddenly wish I had a little more of an emergency kit nested in the back of my car. It's a bad time to need road-side assistance, me being a delicate feminine creature and all. She groans again but settles into a steady rhythm of wheels on pavement. Thump... thump... thump... thump... The rhythm of a stone in the tire alone is nearly enough to send me to the sandman. But I'm not ready for him. It's not time yet. I must travel on.

Dawn brings me to another small speck of existence in the vast no man's land of farm country. I nearly weep with the sight of sun glinting off of dusty chrome and tattered awnings flapping lazily in the breeze. The diner calls my name, promising coffee and various edibles that are guaranteed to stick to my ribs... and most likely give me mild heart burn.

The menu is no disappointment. The sheer amount of fried foods with and without gravy are enough to make my stomach lurch in both joy and disgust. I take my coffee black. Not my typical routine, but right now I'm all business. The waitress doesn't question, she just sloshes a mug full of steaming opaque brown liquid in front of me before I can say 'pie.' Contentment in a cup. I am, for a moment, happy. My hands curl around the steaming mug like it's a life line in a violent, cold sea. A small breath escapes me before I realize my serenity has been once again invaded by the help.

"What'll it be hon?"
"Chicken fried steak."
"Home fries?"
"You bet."

She doesn't even nod or say thank you. She just walks away, pencil once again lodged in Aqua Net encrusted hair. And strangely enough, I'm okay with that. The less contact I have with the outside world today, the better.

My mood turns gray as my bleary gaze focuses on the dew silently being ravaged by the rising sun. There is a lot of unwanted road between me and my homeland. I don't want to do this but I can't bury the gnawing draw this time. I know better yet I refused to fight it. Going against your gut is always the first mistake.

The chirp of a tire breaks my trance and I suddenly feel vulnerable. Coffee slipping through my lips gives me the time I need to regain my composure as I pretend to study the depth and sophistication of the brew to an elemental level. A ten gallon hat with painted on Levi's strolls up to the breakfast counter to a waiting cup of hot black lava. He pretends not to notice me. I pretend not to notice him pretending not to notice me. The place is empty and isolated; anyone who didn't realize they had company would be a fool.

Shoulders slump slightly and posture relaxes as he settles onto the familiar stool. Muscle memory at its finest. He traces the rim of the coffee cup, round and round, as if in his own caffeine induced trance, lips slightly parted as shallow breaths come and go. His eyes don't focus on what is in front of him, they merely gaze off into a distant vision that only he can see. A flicker of emotion passes over the otherwise stolid face. His eyes dart and head drops as if he is suddenly very aware and acknowledging that he's not alone. Finally the curiosity gets the best of him and he glances my way, hoping not to get caught looking but knowing that he will. The dance has begun.

My mouth stays in a thin line but my eyes lock on him long enough to exchange the slightest nod and then go back to my coffee cup chemistry. But the spell has been broken- the fine hairs on the back of my neck tingling betray that.

I only get caught 'not looking' one more time... that I know of. In my peripheral vision I see the hand go for the pocket, a blurry shape of green floats to the counter and with a whisk, he's gone. A trail of dust floating in the hazy morning is all that remains.

My fingers idly turn the edge of my thin paper napkin into a flurry of fringe and confetti while I once again drift off in to the gray. I mull over calling my sister for a status report and decide against it. I'll get there when I get there. Space and time will not keep events from unfolding just because they're inconvenient to me.

At the last second I manage to keep from jumping

out of my skin as a hot ceramic plate slaps down on the table in front of me, crashing into my now empty coffee cup.

"Ketchup?" she grunts. I nod dumbly, only to receive a sticky bottle which has clearly been refilled so many times that the label is impossible to decipher. Consequently, I avoid inspecting my silverware too closely. Some things are best left ignored.

The liquid hot gold reappears in my cup as I saw through the deep fried, gravy laden shoe leather. At least the seasoning is somewhat redeeming. I hate bland shoe leather. The jab from my jacket pocket as I saw goads me to stay on course. I pull the map out so I can multitask while chewing diligently on my meal.

The route ahead reveals that I made better time than expected, despite my inconvenient pit stop the evening before. Driving all night has me ahead of schedule though my aching eyes aren't nearly as happy about that as the rest of my body. If I maintain my pace I can be there by dusk. My heart shoots a burst of flight through my body at the prospect, but my brain overrules.

The car, like a magnet, once again draws my gaze and a heavy sigh. Gas is getting low and my mileage is in dire need of improvement. Nothing is ever easy.

My elbow slips on a piece of paper, scrawled with the words 'special,' 'joe' and a number that more closely resembles an ancient rune than a tab. I settle up the bill and walk into the restroom to wash my face, in a desperate attempt to increase my alertness. Voices in the distance make my ears perk but the running water manages to drown out anything of value. I glance at my watch like it matters and straighten myself up for the trip ahead, reciting a mental pep talk as I glance in the mirror one last time.

You can do this. Deep breaths. It will be over soon and things can go back to normal. Another deep breath and I stroll out of the restroom, heading straight for the door.

"You know..." a voice drawls, giving me time to acknowledge that it is addressing me. "If you're low on gas, you're going to want to fill up at the next station you see. The three after that have been dry for months, you won't find any luck out there."

"Thanks, I'll keep that in mind," I mumble. Immediately I wonder if someone was getting a little too friendly with my car while I was out of sight. My mind spins scenarios like that, even on a normal day. The door woofs a hot blast of air in my face as I pretend not to hurry. I choke back a grimace and head for my noble steed.

The car is already a sauna. *A pox on roll down windows!* I can feel myself melting in the time it takes to stretch across the seat to the opposite crank, praying for some blessed cross ventilation. A knock on the windows makes me flinch, forcing the seat belt buckle to jab into my already aching body. Daggers stare out of my driver's seat.

"You forgot your map." The penetrating eyes wave my folded and creased square of study material tauntingly.

"Thanks," I spit out, managing to bite back the venom of being caught off guard. My arm shoots out the window, fingers demanding the precious parchment. All too slowly the map lowers to my hand level, stopping short.

"You know... it's going to be a scorcher today. You might want to get a jug of water when you stop, too." He takes a minute to survey my vehicular albatross and shoots me a knowing glance from the glinting grays. "Just in case."

I smile civilly. I can do that sometimes. It's too hard fighting off a starry shine from his belt buckle catching me square in the cornea, I can't avoid squinting as

I stare up at his outline. It's impossible to read his face.

"Thank you. Good advice." I stretch out my palm once again and receive my precious paper without a fight. A small sigh escapes my lips. We both pretend not to notice. "I best be off now. Thanks." My hands slide the keys into the ignition as my eyes play chicken with him, waiting for him to take a step back and clear my path for leaving. He hesitates for a moment, unabashed, but finally starts to retreat. Another civil smile through gritted teeth, a courtesy wave, and I'm on my way.

It takes a full five minutes of watching my rear view before I stop cursing myself out. The road's only reply is the thump, thump, thump of my tire. Next stop, I'm getting that stupid stone out. Waves of snapping static hang in the air as I roll down the road, tweaking the dial with increasing fits of rage.

...was an American gir--... I give up.

Bleached out billboards of eras past inform me now that my fuel stop is up ahead, and that I should honk if I can't stop. I'm sure that never gets old. Pavement has not yet made it to anything beyond the primary roads here. The car is covered in a settling cloud of silty brown and gold as I roll to a stop. I can feel the grime sticking to my moist face and neck, but resist the urge to rub at it. I hover in the small patch of shade from the rusted out pump canopy as the sale numbers flip over in tune with the chugging gas pump. The attendant is doing his best to stay in the shade of the overhangs as well while he busies himself with straightening up the place that no one of any importance is ever bound to see. I guess you have to keep yourself busy in a place like this.

My car is getting baked by the high sun. This is not a good thing. I wrap my refueling, grab a jug of coolant and shove a fist full of slightly damp, crumpled bills into his hand. Another exercise in civility and I'm back en route, eyes open for a nice shady grove and a few moments of peace.

Miles and miles pass with nothing more than scrub brush and dust in my rear view. Even the stripes in the few segments of paved road I find have been faded and ground away from years of neglect and elemental abuse. The occasional stray car passes by, sunglasses glinting behind the film covered windshields. This unseasonable hot streak comes at the end of a miserable dry spell and is downright oppressive to those like myself, without the climate controlled comforts that modern automotive engineering has to offer.

More particles wafting up from my less than solid floor boards, only aggravates the situation. A mirage of heat simmering above the sparse highway reveals a glimmer of shady relief upon the horizon. Hope dictates that my eyes aren't starting to play tricks on me.

A crest of lazily winding road exposes the oasis my tired eyes have been hungering for. The large trees swaying in the sporadic breeze are all I need for a chance to unburden myself from some road weary exhaustion.

Bessie grunts to a halt at the end of a small pull-off close to the lacy trees. Letting my eyes shift and refocus, I realize a grove of willows is what beckoned me from the radiating pavement. Water hungry trees... excellent. There might even be a little trickle of a spring seeping through the stand that I can take advantage of.

At the car I rifle though my jacket pockets, wishing I had grabbed a packet of crackers or even ketchup from my last stop. It's well after lunch time and I'm without sustenance. The irony of people purposefully starving themselves skinny makes me snort. A half melted stick of gum lodges itself under my fingernails in the darkness of the linty pocket. It will have to do.

The peppermint tingle does manage to refresh my spirit, if only for a flavor bursting moment. I wander down the tree line, in search of some moist ground and a soft, cool place to rest my eyes. I curse myself for only grabbing the coolant for the car, and not a bottle of coolant for my own personal use. More stupid mistakes.

A nice root system on some less than rocky dirt seems to be my best options for relaxation. A heavy groan escapes me involuntarily as I lean into the semi-cool ground. *My map. Shit.* Still sitting there on the dash, it wrinkles in the wind, waving at me. It can stay there for another minute, I'm not ready to get up yet.

The bark of the tree pulls at me roughly as I lean back into the crevices of the trunk. I am unconcerned. An occasional ant or winged woodland pest strays across my skin only to meet its swift end with a flick of the fingernail. I don't even look. I am unfazed. I just want to close my eyes. Just for a minute...

The darkness takes me immediately. The sandman has been waiting for me, scratching at the door for the past hour. All he needed was an opening and I was defenseless. My body crashes hard for ten, fifteen, maybe even twenty minutes. Time is relative at this point. *A Horse With No Name* starts looping in my semi lucid haze. I sink into the caress of a soft breeze, eyelids fluttering in defiance. *Don't stop now. It's not time yet.*

I let out another groan as my brain overrules my subversive body. *You've had your power nap. Get on with it.* My hand chases sticky beads of sweat off my brow, eyes attempting to reawaken and individually refocus across the rolling fields of nothing. For a moment I pause as a glint of sunfire in the distance catches my eye. Company? Passers by? I'm not quite sure if I care. I watch for another minute, trying to recapture the location of the last flash, but to no avail. Best to get on with things.

The trunk latch is always tricky business. The dirt and fine dust from this sun scorched earth is not making matters any easier. After enough jiggling, it gives way, like it always does. The crowbar is my first order of business. It's hot to the touch; not a welcome feeling, but I'll get over it. I trace the tire treads with my fingers until I find the offending stone that has been trying to lull me in to a slumber with its hypnotic rhythms. A single stone is no match for my tapered bar of steel. I go over the rest of the tires, just for good measure. Wouldn't want to get back on the road and find I had an encore lurking in the wings.

Then there's the matter of the extra cargo, which I really don't feel like handling at this point in the day. The heat and motion have not been kind and I'd rather not mess up my good gloves. The clearing, as it stands, looks like it will afford me ample room to negotiate a turn around to get Bessie closer to the tree line. At least this will spare my back a little extra work. Plus it's bad manners to dump such trash in a clearing as nice as this.

The car easily glides into place and I re-pop the trunk. It's less disgruntled after the previous foreplay. Unloading and not making an obvious mess takes some time. Amazing how gritting your teeth seems to make heavy lifting so much easier. Smiling just doesn't have the same impact. Maybe it's the presence of mind, the mental focus, I'm not one to say. All I know is that it works and soon my aching jaw has the issue resolved.

Concealing the heap of trash isn't worth the time I would usually take. Sometimes the badlands have their own advantages. I give the pile of crap a final kick for good measure. After all this hassle it does make me feel a little better.

The car eases smoothly up on to the road now. The overloaded bounce is gone and I'm happier for the better handling. Even the radio agrees and settles on a station without proclamation of hellfire and Dalmatians. Damnation, I mean, of course... but I can't help snicker to myself every time I hear it. Bible thumping is clearly a very serious industry in these parts. The end of times is not my concern. I'll meet my maker on my own terms.

It only takes a half mile or so before I catch another glint of shiny glass in my mirrors. It's too soon. The air warped with heat makes it hard to discern what exactly is trolling behind me. Sometimes the vapors make it look like a truck, other times it looks like a sports car. In reality it could be nothing at all. Time passes and the shape doesn't change position. I cease worrying.

My little power nap and heavy garbage disposal took longer than intended, but the body can only be pushed so far before it breaks.

-4-

I could never keep a hairbrush. It just wasn't practical. A nice boar hair bristle would be laid to waste in a week if it was the closest thing on hand near me or my siblings. It wasn't that children were rough on things. It was how the sturdy head cracked against young flesh once enough force was imparted. We were to be schooled. We were to be loved in a godly manner. "Spare the rod, spoil the child." Righteous and Holy, the hand of the Lord spoke through the bristles that He created in His good mercy.

It took all too long before I realized that I had two options: dreads or buzz cuts. Tempting as it was to Rasta-fy my look, my flesh wasn't up to the consequences.

I cut my hair the day I turned fourteen. Nothing left to grab on to, nothing left to pull, nothing left to brush. Some days I still wonder why it didn't occur to any one of us sooner. But logic is lost on most fourteen year olds. Survival skills are not. Chastise. Mock. It didn't matter. What mattered was the ground they had lost and I had gained. Words hurt far less than the sticks and stones and wood spoons that I was used to. A hurled insult was like a blessed rain. Call me unholy names. Scream until your nostrils trickle blood. It was always far easier to make excuses for defamation than it was bruises. Blend in with the disenfranchised, no one would even think twice. It's the cool thing to do, others would understand without really knowing, pretending they can relate. Don't draw attention to the real plight at hand though, no one really wants to be inconvenienced with reality. In the long run, flesh heals quicker than spirit. These are lessons that we only learn the hard way.

They both scar. Some are just easier to see than others.

Measures could be taken to forget the pain, to control the angst, to block out the shadows at your threshold. A slender blade; small, shiny and honed to perfection allowed an escape again and again from the darkness that lurked outside my door at night.

The pacing. The waiting. Knowing that eventually, I would be weak and alone. The Sandman tapping at my door was the one knock I couldn't fight, couldn't resist. Silent in the night there was no need to hurry, to rush. The audience that doesn't realize they could leave. Evils crept upon the shadows, feeding in the darkness, satisfying things that could not be justified in the light of day. There was always time. Plenty of time.

Marks that left patterns in my being could be traced and relived again and again, when things reeled out of control. Fingers tracing ancient paths of experience. Some days I still catch myself tracing the trails of suffering in ritualistic patterns. Habit drew my fingers along the lines, the paths of pain. Memories of the past flashing forward like a highlight reel through my mind's eye.

Remembering one sin in order to forget another, again and again and again. Weakness bears empowerment. A faint gasp of color in a field of gray.

A burning glare in my eye brings me back to conscious awareness of my current situation. The dusty chrome grill of a large truck looms at me, drifting carelessly across the poor excuse for a center line at a rise in the open road. Clearly he is not used to having any company on this stretch of forsaken highway and I'm soon to pay the price for daydreaming. A hard swerve right takes me out of this path of travel, a hard lay on the horn does nothing. The car grinds over the rough berm kicking up clouds of dust and rocks, worn down tires resisting my evasive maneuvers. A fishtail later I'm under control and exploring my dictionary of exotic curses.

Throbbing pulses in my eardrums fade long enough for the grinding sound of steel on pavement to raise the hair on the back of my neck. Tires. Shit. A four point inspection was not on my itinerary. Unbelievable.

Squinting doesn't make the problem go away. No matter how much I try to blur them out and envision a tire, the chewed up steel mocks me. Of course, the radio still works. At least there's that.

I appreciate the moment of irony that washes over me as I once again coerce the now empty trunk open.

Waist deep in the stale cavern, searching for the medieval torture device that auto manufacturers call a jack, I don't hear the wheels ease up behind me. The slam of a truck door sends my head in to the metal. Perfect.

"What tha-..." My spin only reveals a cloud of dust settling behind me. I catch a glimpse of hat and buckle. *You've got to be kidding me.*

"Run in to some trouble?" The Ten Gallon Hat swaggers up to me.

"Oh, you know, the usual. I like to time myself on my tire changing capabilities so someday I can try out for a NASCAR pit crew and live the dream."

He smirks.

"Nasty bit of business you got there." I could hear the chivalrous judgment suck through his teeth.

"It's not a problem." The rusty metal jack is useless without the handle that still eludes me.

"Got a spare?" He saunters forward, cuffing his sleeves.

"No. Really. It's fine. I got it." The snap in my tone doesn't keep him from coming dangerously close to invading my personal space.

"That may well be, but I couldn't leave you in the dust in good conscience. It's not in my nature."

It's becoming abundantly clear that the quickest way to get rid of him is to keep him busy on the tire and not sniffing around the rest of my stuff.

"Fine," I exhale, throwing in a pointed eye roll for effect. "Here's the tire iron. Feel free to bust some nuts loose while I find the rest of this tetanus trap." I throw the iron at his feet.

"Eeeeeeasy. I'm just trying to help." He stoops to claim the iron and heads towards the offending wheel. I turn back to the trunk and continue my search. The far corner yields the gnarled rubber grip of a jack handle. I shove the rest of the stray contents deeper into the dark recesses.

Tugging on the spare is futile. It's not seen the light of day in the span of my ownership and it's not eager to give up a long-standing resting place. Push. Pull. Wiggle. Nothing. I swear I can hear the Universe laughing on the wind. Mocking bitch.

My spirit breaks, ready to seek help, as it finally jumps loose and, dumps me flat on my ass. A snicker leaks out from the far side of my car but is quickly muffled. A prompt dusting off and back to my task, praying the spare has enough air left in it to get me anywhere but here. This must be what hell feels like, mostly the inane torture level. The threat of repeating this every day of the afterlife is almost enough to scare me straight.

Almost.

With a final clink of lug nut in hub cap the eager help has the busted out rim off in time for me to roll around the replacement. He's almost useful.

Almost.

Small talk is kept to a minimum. Maybe it's the scowl or the dark circles under my eyes that tell him I'm not in the mood for sharing. When I find myself almost appreciating the help, I know I must be tired.

"There ya go," he dusts off those painted on Levi's, surveying his work carefully. "That should hold you till you get to the next town at least. It's not far up and there's a decent little garage there too if you want to have your full size replaced."

"Great. Um... thanks." Suddenly I'm awkward. One of the things I do best.

"No problem. I'll even follow you in to town to make sure you get there okay."

Wait. What?

"Uhh, no really, that's not necessary. She looks fine. I can handle it." People need to get too close, even if it is just to my fender.

"Oh it's no problem. I'm on my way through anyhow." He dips his hat and heads back for the truck. The lack of control of the situation normally would send me into combative mode but I'm just too damn tired to care.

-6-

Town isn't too far down the road and looks like a nice speck of civilization in the middle of farm country. Rarely am I happy to see a chain or big box store, but sometimes they fill a need for the familiar. Today I am not disappointed. Big box retail for the win.

My knight in dusty armor gets me oriented and surprisingly doesn't hover. The fleeting sensation of disappointment is quickly replaced with the desire to swoon the moment the cool air conditioning of the vestibule greets my skin with a cold slap. Typically I hate air conditioning. Today is one of the rare exceptions.

Droning overhead lights and the chirp of a cart wheel squeaking in the distance serenade me as I wrangle myself up a new wheel, a cold beverage, a pile of snacks and a family-size pack of wet-naps. I'm tired of being sticky, those will have to do. My cash isn't going to make it as far as I'd anticipated at this rate; hopefully this trip doesn't run in to any further complications.

Twenty minutes to kill until they can fix up my baby's shoes. It's too damn hot to explore the local scene so I settle into the store cafe, something I'd never do under normal circumstances. Ever. Never ever. At this

point I'm not surprised to see Mr. Levi's filtering through the check out. Of course.

Thinking too loud draws his attention and he meets my gaze with a quick smile and shrug. Not looking away fast enough unwittingly extends and invitation for company. More lessons in civility. Fantastic.

"So, how long are ya in for?"

Not comprehending the words before me, I stare at him dumbly. Surprise awkwardness yet again. One more strike and I'm out.

"...the car." He motions. "How long will it take?"

Cheeks run red at my simple oversight. I curse myself for looking like a fool without trying to be obvious.

"Oh. Only twenty minutes or so. Apparently there's not a lot going on around here." My eyes survey the scenery of the empty store. "Whoever could imagine. Lucky me." My nostrils flare at the scent of irony served cold.

"Well this isn't a bad place to be if you're in a jam. They have pretty good resources compared to the rest of the towns on this route. You are one lucky lady, maybe there's a guardian angel looking after you."

The only angel I need is one that can tell me how to outrun the devil. The rest can take their halos and harps and... I manage to shake off the internal musing and keep it from stumbling out of my lips. Score one for me.

"So... What brings you through town?" The quirked eyebrows suggest that I was not only silent for too long, but that I've also been too accommodating.

"Other than an ill timed flat tire? Business. Family. A search for adventure. The usual." I'm hoping it's a good enough answer. It's not. He tries for more banter, more small talk. I manage to keep him occupied while not revealing anything useful. I should have been a politician, Lord knows I have enough skeletons in my closet. Maybe I *would* be qualified. The eye twinkle across the table is mildly distracting but not bewitching. I know better. He thinks he's getting more information out of me than I want him to have. He's wrong.

Matching parry to thrust kills a considerable amount of time and before I know it the crackling voice of God... the loudspeaker for the store, requests my presence at the service desk to pick up my car. Thank goodness for small miracles. Payment settled, I take a quick spin around my rusty chariot, making sure nothing is out of place. She's solid once again. As solid as she's going to get at least, and ready for the road. I wish I could say the same for myself. All I want is rest. Rest just plain isn't going to happen in the near future. I'll sleep when I'm dead.

Car loaded and eager to run, my body still feels heavy and lethargic. The brief bout of air conditioning and hydration did refresh the wilting pile of flesh pouring into the driver's seat. I try to say polite goodbyes, but what do you say when politeness and the desire to gnaw your arm off to escape are at odds with each other?

"I'm off. Thanks for the help." I avoid eye contact, it only drags things out.

"Good luck, have a safe trip. Maybe I'll see you around." He smiles, going for that last bit of charm.

"I sure hope not," slips out of my lips as I slam the door. I see his head swivel, trying to decipher my parting words. I force a toothy smile and slam on the gas.

I have to get off of this godforsaken road.

Too many complications and not enough time are turning a simple drive into an endurance challenge. The witching hour is a wonderful time for long lost homecomings. The thought of it does make me snort with amusement.

The sun hangs lazily on the horizon, offering up the first few breaths of relief from its solar oppression. I can breathe again. The car flying down the road, windows open, has my hair standing up on end while my skin prickles from the coolness. It feels good. So good. The further the sun droops, the colder the sting of wind on my face. I leave the windows down until I'm numb. The cold distracts my busy mind. Focusing on the increasing discomfort keeps my thoughts from reliving past transgressions that lead me here. An old trick that's rarely let me down.

The road is smooth and quiet for once. I can settle in to a nice groove and make up some time; a couple hundred miles and I'll be reaching the city limits. I am not eagerly anticipating the arrival. Funny how at one age, something you vehemently vowed against becomes something you're craving to do later in life.

My family. I tried to remove myself from them. All of them. Little sister kept track of me though. Little sister didn't have the same childhood that I did, else she would have better understood.

Little Lacey May. Apple of daddy's eye. She was the youngest, after all; that always helped. To my knowledge she bore the least amount of abuse from the boorish bastard. Then again, I didn't stick around long enough to find out. Lacey kept track of me when she got older, in a desperate attempt to keep the family together. Her memories were fonder than mine. Sometimes I tried to tell her, most times I kept it to myself. It wasn't worth wasting my breath. A solid ten years stood between Lacey and me. Ten years was a world of difference.

Lacey had long, golden hair that shone like the sun and fell in perfect ringlets. She was my polar opposite. Somewhere along the line the recessive genes finally got a chance to mix between our parents, to the point the later children didn't personify the aura of freak that was our family crest of shame. I always envied that. Lacey was the only one to stay after she was eighteen. She worked at a small paint-your-own pottery shop after school each day, dolling out lady bugs and garden gnomes to over scheduled soccer moms and neurotic home-schoolers.

She was smart. Very smart. But being the last in the line of a big family did her no favors at the financial aid

office. There were no other dependents; she was essentially an only child that was too bright for her own good. She made do with part time community college classes while she scraped together her pennies from hand crafts, odd jobs and an occasional stint pet sitting. She had always seemed to prefer animals to babies; sometimes she was awkward with the small writhing humans. I couldn't fault her for that. She didn't grow up playing nursemaid to them like I did.

Sometimes she would call and look for some sisterly advice on boys, glazes or how to hang a picture. I liked our conversations for that. They were eclectic. You never quite knew what you would be getting in to when you picked up the phone, but it was generally entertaining if not thought-provoking coming from one so young. She would be great if she could find the right wardrobe to walk though. All it would take was a good break - I knew she could take care of the rest.

The problem with Lacey was that she was too nice. That was more of a weakness in dealing with our family than most. She tried to be peacemaker. She didn't like it when people fought. This was one of the main reasons she tried so desperately to keep in contact with me all these years. She couldn't accept that we were flawed. That we were broken.

The rose colored glasses always evoked ire in me quicker than a harsh slap. I feared she would be taken advantage of, used, exploited if the wrong opportunity arose. Once there was a boy in school. They were madly in love, as most throbbing hormonal teenagers tend to be. He told her pretty things in the shadows of the night. They would sneak away to steal moments behind the honeysuckle and roses. He wanted her. He needed her. And she felt the same.

She called me the night she was planning to run away with him. She made me swear to write down my mother's number. I had done my best to disavow any knowledge of family contacts. She pleaded. I promised. I didn't want her to worry.

The word 'elope' rang out in my ear. I tried to protest, but it was useless. I sighed and listened. Young love often feels bittersweet to outside observers. Memories of those lost in the pursuit of a greater life, a greater plan, still sting when fresh faced optimism enthusiastically babbles on.

You want to warn them, but you can't. It's like watching someone standing on the train tracks, hearing the whistle blow in the distance of the dark night. Keep your eyes open dear, keep an ear to the ground. When you feel the earth rumble under your feet, be ready to save yourself. *Be ready,* you whisper as she hangs up the phone.

Days passed. No news from the happy couple. No irate calls from family members who shouldn't have my number anyhow. Maybe she had made it. Maybe she had crossed the tracks without harm. I secretly hoped for her that she did.

It took two weeks before I found myself picking up the phone, only to find a sobbing mass of echoes pouring through the receiver. He hadn't come. He never showed. Their sweet plans fell to shredded little tatters of a heart. She couldn't understand. Time and time again she insisted that it wasn't right, that something must have happened. I listened and kept the knowing sighs to myself. There would be a time later when she would be ready. That time wasn't now.

His parents told her he left town; without her, leaving only a note in the night. They hadn't seen him since. Heartbreak is hard enough to heal when you're face to face, let alone over miles of buried wire and conduit. She would grieve, she would move on. This I knew. Human nature was a fickle yet resilient mistress we can never escape. Lift us up only to let us fall, and then lets us once again rise from the ashes. The cycle churns on for seventy or eighty years before coming to a typically lackluster end in a facility that smells of stale urine and tapioca.

Life sucks. Then you die. Then you decompose. Some days that simple fact was the only thing that kept me going. No one gets out of this life alive. Morbid pragmatism was what I did best. It kept me company on cold winter nights, but it didn't keep me warm.

Little Lacey would be looking for me soon. I couldn't help but grimace, already feeling the pangs of her disappointment across my chest. She would stay up, she would wait. She would have a pot of chamomile steeping for me after a long, arduous drive. I should call her, but the highway lights blur by too easy. It's better to make up the time. She'll understand.

Lacey had a small apartment with two cats, an iguana, and a hedgehog only a few blocks south of the family homestead. She liked to be close but her innate love for animals necessitated the need for her own space. Father had always been allergic. No furry friends for us. Not for long at least. Those few that did get smuggled in under his stringent watch often met a tragic end. Rodent to reptile, they all incurred the same wrath. It didn't take long before we quit trying. Our house was no sanctuary to any living creature.

I agreed to stay with her when she had first called. It was the safest place I could be without having to shell out extra money for accommodations. It might be nice. I hadn't seen much of her as a grown woman, so I was curious yet prepared to be disgusted by her natural beauty. Damn kid had it all.

-9-

Time distorts after a sleepless night and the hypnotizing miles of payment. I don't remember the miles, they simply float by as if I'm in a dream. For a second I question myself, hoping that I didn't breeze through a traffic situation of dire importance. How many bunnies had suffered from my wheels while I daydreamed? There is no way to know.

The familiar glow of the roadside food stop catches my attention and snaps me out of my trance. I guess once the golden arches set up residence, it's not prone to change. I shake off an unwilling chill as I pass into what could only be the outskirts of my home town. I feel like I've been teleported as I realize not only the temperature but the scenery has changed. The cold blush of fall is on the air. This is an unpleasant realization that comes to me entirely too late; I should have planned better.

The bag in my back seat was not packed for a multi-season experience, as was likely in my homeland. I was at once happy and sad that this innate knowledge had left me. I didn't need the maps from here on out; instinct took over. Some of the landmarks had changed with the passage of time but the basic landscape was still identifiable.

As the streets and alleys I once called home pass by, I can't help but recount the memories of my youth. The first place I was kissed. The first place I smoked a cigarette. The first place I learned I could get my booze under age. The place I got my first black eye. Yes, I was home.

I drive slowly, taking in the scenery of the street in front of me, painted sickly yellow in the street lights. Tainted and tinged colors, like my memories, fade in the background.

The house.

I'm not sure what to think. It's not nearly as sad as I expect it to be. As I *want* it to be. The paint is peeling and the shutters hang limp with the passage of time, but outwardly it doesn't betray the life lead within it. I am disappointed.

I feel my jaw clench as I round the block, heading to Lacey's. The pain shoots through my temple before I realize what I'm doing.

Stop. Mind over matter. Be immune to the pain. Block it out. Soon it won't matter. Be still. Breathe.

The car turns, slowing on to my sister's avenue. I remember this place faintly. I pull up to a small duplex. You wouldn't even have to tell me to know which one was hers. Flower boxes spill forth fragrant viney blooms in the night, caressing gnomes and goblins of the most vibrant colors, even in the faded street light. Pinwheels and glass fireflies waiting to be lit by the sun adorn the walkway leading up to her door. I can see a light on, probably the kitchen. I can only hope she's still awake, if not it's going to be another rough night for me and the car.

I knock. Gently at first. It feels like the rapping of my knuckles echoes through the entire neighborhood of darkness. No response. No sign of stirring. It's to be expected. The second time I am more forceful, more intent. Before long I hear shuffling and china clattering from behind the door. At least someone is home and now awake, hopefully it's the right person.

Time passes quickly but feels like ages when you're standing exposed, surrounded by the shadows. Finally I hear a bolt slide in the door. And a lock. And another lock. Can't be too safe, you never really know what devil is at your doorstep. My palms dampen, waiting for the door knob to turn.

Lacey stands there, resplendent in her flannel pajamas and perfectly disheveled bed head, hand knit shawl drawn tight over her shoulders.

"Anna!" she squeals, leaping on to me in a big bear hug. Several moments pass before I can wrangle myself free and take a full breath.

"Hey there, kiddo. Sorry I'm late... car trouble." I cast a telling nod over my shoulder.

"Oh don't worry, don't worry. I knew you'd come! I tried to wait up but..." she looks guilty. "I guess I drifted off..." A stiff autumn breeze comes through making us suddenly aware that this was a conversation better had in the comfort of a home. She shudders at the chill, casting her eyes up into the clear, cold sky, seeming to focus on things that only she can see. I glance up too, trying to focus but see nothing but the traces of my breath.

I roll up the windows, securing my car the best I can. The moon is full and chases us indoors with the promise of frost. In recent years the neighborhood has fallen into disrepair, not that it was affluent to begin with. Lower middle class gave way to thugs, squatters and low income palaces of despair. They had tried to establish a patrolling neighborhood watch but eventually dirt and intimidation had won out.

Lacey has tea waiting for me. It's tepid now. That's my fault. She offers to warm it up for me. It's too soon for me to be a bother but on this night a little warmth inside is welcome. I sit down at the table like a deflated balloon. It's funny how being in a car for so long makes you want to go relax and sit down.

I size her up for a moment as she moves around her kitchen. A sudden pressure against my calf makes me jump until I realize it's purring at me. I shoo it away quietly. I'm not in the mood to be friends right now.

Lacey got the looks in the family. All the odds and ends that made up our quirks came together in a perfect canvas with her. Delicate cheek bones, long blond curly hair, naturally athletic build that seemed to sway in the wind. Sometimes two wrongs can make a right.

It was a puzzle to me as to why she was still alone. She was creative, she was ambitious, she was beautiful and she was kind. It had been years since her Romeo had left her crying in the honeysuckle; I couldn't and didn't believe she was still holding a torch for him.

"So what's the status?" I was tired but I got down to business.

"She's in and out at this point. Oxygen, IV's, you name it. She's in and out of ICU every other day it seems. They can't put a finger on it but they think it was a series of mini strokes." She looks upset. I don't.

"Did you call the others?"

"Yes, of course. Took a while to get a hold of them but the rest should be here tomorrow. You're the first." I manage a nod.

Great. At least that affords me a bit of time to get my bearings, but not much. Time to build the fortress high and prepare for survival mode.

"Well sis, thanks for the tea. It's been a long, long drive. If you don't mind..."

"Oh! Of course! I have the sofa all made up for you." She looks apologetic. "I hope you don't mind..."

"Nah, it's fine." I pick up my bag. She points me toward the bathroom, the living room and a big fluffy blanket. The pillow feels like heaven to my tired aching head. The last thing I remember is a heavy sigh of relief.

-10-

Morning comes too quickly. The sun, despite barely peeking through the sheer lace curtains, still manages to cast a beam directly into my pupil. I stir, unwilling to face the day. My body has not rested long enough and lets me know it. Even my bones feel old. The smell of java wafting into my nose catches my attention. My stomach tells me I should get up to investigate. My head tells me I should just lay here a bit longer. Eyelids flutter and close, conspiring against me until I realize that voices are emanating from the tiny excuse for a kitchen. Once sleepy eyes fly open, surmising just who might be waiting around the doorway. I'm momentarily thankful as I realize I slept in my clothes. It makes morning meetings much less awkward.

Quietly I step towards the kitchen, ears straining for more clues.

"...well the ringmaster said I could have the week off until we were ready to head to the next site, so I'm in no hurry..."

Silver.

Sylvia "Silver" Grey Shaw was a free spirit from birth. When she was three years old she cast off the bonds of her good Christian name and began to insist that everyone call her "Silver." It stuck. As she grew, my favorite cohort evolved in to a willowy figure laden in arts and interpretive dance. She was desperately brilliant but chose to spend her time naked amongst the tress as often as possible. She was a sprite brought to life in the modern age.

Lacey had told me that in recent years Silver had joined up with a dance troupe, mainly touring in the southwest. The weather was nice and the money was adequate. It was hard to make a life as a performer. Silver could master almost any instrument she was given, and could often be found on her off hours playing on street corners and subway stops, augmenting her starving artist income.

As adolescents we ebbed and flowed between best friends and bitter enemies. When I left, I left on the latter terms. We did not stay in touch. Lacey, family archivist, had made sure to keep me up to speed on her progress through the years. I listened with mild curiosity and frequent disgust. Silver did not play by societal norms, and didn't bother pretending to. This gave her a number of run-ins over the years with law enforcement, wives, and even the occasional jealous husband. Her stint at the Tantric training center was one of the more colorful tales I had heard from Lacey, and I'm sure she edited the content to make it more palatable.

"Well, well, well... Silver Grey..." I lean around the corner of the doorway. A face of heavy eyeliner and glitter meets me. It's too early for glitter and charcoal. My sandy eyes protested grumpily.

"Anna." My name shoots out short, clipped and succinct. I bristle.

"Anna! You're up! Here, I made some muffins and the coffee is almost done..." she shoves a plate at me, always the peacemaker. Hard to say something stupid with a muffin in your mouth.

"What's with the war paint? Just get back from a raiding party?" I motion towards Silver with my newly acquired muffin. Lacey's shoulders slump, her attempt to dissipate the tension defeated.

"If you must know, I had to leave the encore presentation of *Madame Swan's Erotic Fantastique* early to make it here," she snorts. "I didn't have time to change," she adds with a dramatic toss of the hair.

"Ah, *burlesque* now, is it?" She nods. I hold back any remaining comments to avoid ruffling her petticoats. I haven't had my coffee yet. As if reading my mind, the blessed pot beeps, letting out a final glug of fresh brewed delight. Lacey already has the mismatched, handmade mugs out with cream and sugar at the ready. That's my girl.

I'm a full cup in before I realize my furry friend is at it again. I'm too tired to fight. Soon I have a purring puddle of happy nestled in my lap. She's warm, I don't mind. Lacey and Silver continue to banter about costumes, lovers, the best place to buy garters and things like authentic silk stockings. I peer at them through sleep deprived eyes, unamused.

"James should be here by noon and Bobby by two." Lacey informs me.

"What about Stephen?" Silver inquires without missing a beat.

"I... I'm not sure he's coming. He had to work." She adds meekly.

I came and Stephen didn't? This seems odd. I don't get a chance to ponder before Silver is back on topic about her crazy sexy glamorous life on the road, *en troupe*. A different venue every night, professionally and personally. She lives for the novelty. I check my watch. It's only nine. Shit.

A shower gives me a good excuse to bow out of girl time. The heat caresses my aching muscles, the steam clouding the senses and giving them a pleasant rest. Spirits revived, I make a plan. Dodge the sisters, head out to the town for a little scenery scouting. Deftly I maneuver the deal and slip out the door, free of the sisterly bond once again. I can relax.

I close my eyes, back safe in my fortress of solitude. Imagination runs through the thoughts and memories of the past. Where to go? What to see? Does it matter? No, it doesn't. Does my curious nature need to be fed? Yes, it does.

-11-

Many of the old traffic patterns are the same. I give way to my old driving habits and before long find myself back at our old school. The anger that flushes through my skin is immediate. My hatred for this farce of an institution has not dulled over the years. Bastard kids. Bastard teachers. Bastard administration. No one helped. No one stepped in. No one even tried to understand. I should have burned that fucker to the ground the day I left its unconsecrated grounds.

I circle the school, seething from past injustice, shocked at how quickly it all comes flooding back. They shouldn't have mocked me. They never believed what I was capable of. My jaw clenches as I notice a side gymnasium door, slightly ajar. I'm nothing, if not tempted.

Bessie blends easily in to the teacher's lot in this dead end town. It would be hard to pick her out of the crowd. Somehow, this is depressing. I venture towards the school, keeping an eye out for monitors of any kind. In a terrorist happy world, many knee jerk security measures have been put in place. Bright neon signs posted around the area spout off instructions about checking in at the office, getting a visitor ID, not being on school grounds

during operating hours... Their Gestapo tactics are so cute. In I walk. Under the radar. It feels so insubordinate. One step inside and... no one's there. *Balls.*

Silence follows me down the halls, as I recall when and where I was as my pre-adulthood was formed. Many things had changed, shifted, been refaced over the years. It's to be expected; evolution is fluid. Times change.

I turn the corner to find a familiar set of eyes staring at me. This stops me dead in my tracks. Cue the tumbleweed and the wild west whistle.

"Ma'am you can't be her-...wait... Do I know you? An-..Anna? Anna Shaw?"

My palms run cold.

"Yes, Clark. Anna. Anna Shaw." Immediately his eyes light up. *What fresh hell is this?*

"Well, hey there! How the hell have you been? It's always great to see an alum in my halls!" He advances. I don't.

"In YOUR halls?" My head shakes in mild disbelief.

"Well yeah, my halls. What, you didn't know I was the Principal of our illustrious Alma Matter now?"

"Uh. No. I must have missed that newsletter..." *Get. Me. Out.* My brain screams. "Well, I was just curious... I guess I'll be going..."

"Oh no, don't worry about it. You're with ME now." He gives me his most dashing wink. I try not to vomit a little in my mouth. "How would you like the executive tour? You can relive our glory days!"

I keep my eyes from narrowing, of this I'm sure. The instinctive nostril flare is slightly harder to control. The scent of prey on the wind is hard to miss.

Clark Gribley, high school Principal. Am I in hell? Did I die and not know it? Was there a wormhole somewhere that I missed? I have to wonder. I follow him down the hall, a scant step behind to monitor where exactly we're headed. The science wing; cutting edge, all new equipment, floor to ceiling displays. He beams. My head nods along, missing the significance of the new marker boards. I feel like I should give him a cookie, but his pot belly suggests one too many stolen from the stashes of the school cafeteria as is.

He touches my elbow ever so lightly and drags me down a hallway I don't remember from our past. Athletics. Fantastic. The well-lit corridor houses trophies from floor to ceiling. I am assured, quite humbly, that this is but the tip of the iceberg. I pretend to be impressed without inquiring. It's the best chance I have to get him to leave me alone, but he doesn't.

Another quick turn and we're out at the football field.

"Ah the glory days," he recalls. "Vim, vigor, virility under the bleachers... *Don't you remember?"*

"No, I don't remember getting felt up under the bleachers, sorry. I guess I must have missed that elective, not being a pom-pom wielding whore and all." My mouth holds a sour pucker I can't fight. I can see his Neolithic brow furrow.

"Well there's no need to be a snot about it," he frowns harder.

"I'm sorry, what? A 'snot'?" I feel my head swivel in bemusement.

"I'm *sorry* but yes. There's no reason to be bitter just because you weren't popular." He seems quite satisfied with his retort.

"Not...*popular?* You think I'm mad because no one tried to knock me up every Friday night when I was sixteen?"

"Now you're just being crass." Clearly someone had been exposed to the Disney channel mentality entirely too long. Time for some adult conversation.

"Look, Clark, I'm sorry to burst your bubble yet

again. Go fuck yourself and thanks for the trip down memory lane, but I really should be going..." I rifle my pocket for keys and begin to step away. There's that hand on my arm again. I freeze.

"I... I didn't mean it that way... It's just that you always seemed so cool, so *counter-culture*." He even uses air quotes for effect. "Thing is..." he masters looking bashful "I always had a crush on you." Uncomfortable silence. "It seems funny now, doesn't it?"

"Yeah. Hilarious. You had a hell of a way of showing it." I cut my retort off only to find myself toe to toe with the now head of our "illustrious institution."

"You know... I always wondered..." his eyes wander up and down, "where it was that you went Junior year... everyone said you left town with a band as a groupie. That sounds sooo cool." A finger reaches out to touch my hair, my hand flies up in reflex.

"What the *hell* do you think you're doing?" It spills forth as a growl. He hesitates but only for a moment.

"Oh come on, Anna. I remember the way you used to look at me. And look at us now, here we are just like old times. One on one, stars aligned." He takes a thoughtful pause. "I always liked you, you know... Despite the rest..." His words hang heavy in the air like they're the most important words that have ever been uttered in history.

I take his deep pause as an opportunity to put some distance between us. The cruelty I suffered at his hands, I can't even begin to explain to him. The taunting, the emotional torture, the... Well, it's enough to drive a girl to cut herself. Among other things.

"Where are you going?" His hand is on my arm again, aroused confusion across his face. The grip tightens as he pulls me close. "Don't you want a second chance at our *glory days?* You've hardly changed a bit..." he whispers, breath hot on my neck.

All it takes is a flash of steel; thumb-studded

Damascus glinting in the autumn sun. Precision has always been a gift. It doesn't take much of a blade to get a reaction. An inch and a half in the right place can stop an argument short abruptly. A hand grabs for my hair in desperation, only to come up empty. It makes me smile. Hot crimson starts to flow, quickly spilling out of the freshly inflicted wound. Things will get messy if not quickly taken care of, and I'm without a change of clothes handy.

My eyes cast about feverishly, looking for a good place to rest before this becomes too difficult. An old concession stand with a close door is opportune. Gravity both helps and hinders my attempt to lead his ever wilting body in that direction, cooing momentary inspirations to keep him going in his disoriented state helps. It's best to move before mobility is impaired. There's no winning a dragging game with this one.

The door, ragged from years of abuse, pops open easily just like it always did. A careful toe maneuver and the metal slab opens far enough for the two of us to slip inside.

He falls like a lump of hot road kill, hitting the floor with a dull thud. The floor shakes. I tug at my shirt errantly, trying to straighten up and take a quick survey of the field. No one around. This makes my job infinitely easier.

The life hasn't fully left his lips yet, but it won't be long until the seeping pool collecting under him drains the final gasps of spirit. I find a paper towel to wipe my knife clean, careful to get any flecks of mortality off myself in the process. I wipe the wound down for good measure. No sense giving forensics any more material than necessary. In a stroke of luck, the concession has a food grinder and compactor. Given more time I might take more liberal advantage of this industrial feature, but for now it's enough to eat a paper towel or two. That is all I need.

Minutes seem like hours before I slip back outside, ears straining for the chime of the class bell. Nothing. I smile and shove my hands in my pockets. It's a leisurely stroll back to the car. I take my time and enjoy the scenery. My stomach grumbles in protest of my abbreviated breakfast. Time to feed another hunger.

Coffee chain. Coffee chain. Coffee chain. Fast food restaurant pretending to be a coffee chain. Donut chain with coffee. These options bore me. I both understand and appreciate that coffee is the opiate of the masses, but must all of it be so average bordering on sub-par? Finally, a little local bistro that appears to be in something that in its previous life housed a shoe store catches my eye.

The local artisan touch does not disappoint. A warm scone and a double shot for the road spells instant refreshment, but the dial on my wrist informs me that it's pushing eleven. I drag my feet a bit longer before relenting to circle back to Lacey's place. The others will be arriving soon. I'd rather not be the last one into the fray.

-12-

There is already a strange car sitting outside when I pull up. The wallpaper of peacenik stickers gives me momentary pause. Only one way to find out.

The front door nudges open easily, free of its locks and shackles. I can hear laughter up the stairs and smell the brownies in the air. The top of the stairs reveals the arrival of another sibling, stuffing his mouth with fresh baked chocolate goodness. No one is paying attention to the stairs.

"Robert Raymond!" I say in my sternest voice. The trio jumps, prepared to scatter, before locking eyes on me. I smile, the slight devilish dimple in my cheek making a rare appearance.

"Anna!" Bobby jumps up to give me a hug. I suspect I'm left with chocolate smudges. Kids.

I haven't seen Bobby Ray since he hit puberty. He grew tall and lanky, like a hippie scarecrow. The wispy soul patch catches my eye; it looks like he's going for full on flower-child. A slouchy knit cap covers his shoulder length hair. By the looks of the stitching, I'm guessing it was hand crafted by Lacey. Flip flops and muddy frayed cuffs meet the floor. Someone should tell him it's cold outside.

"Anna, Bobby Ray got here right after you left. We figured we had some time to kill until you got back, so he helped us make some *brownies*," she flushes slightly, unsure what my reaction might be. A quirked eyebrow is my only reply.

"C'mon, try one." Robert hands me a gooey square. "They're still waaaaaarm." I could use something to take the edge off.

"Don't mind if I do..."

I'm on the floor trying to accurately reconstruct the previous hour in my own head. All I know is that my abs hurt from laughing too much and there are tortilla chips all over Lacey's floor. Silver is dressed in an outfit made entirely from scarves. I'm not sure how it holds together but I resist the urge to tug at one of them. I have the sneaking suspicion they're meant to drop with a single pull. No thanks.

Bobby sits contentedly in full lotus. It seems natural to him. I look to the kitchen where Lacey is stuck staring vacantly into a cupboard, looking for what I have no idea. Eventually she sighs in defeat and closes the door, padding back to our little circle.

"I'm out of Pringles. Sorry." She looks truly remorseful. I manage not to giggle.

The haze has barely begun to clear when the door bell chimes, sending us to the ceiling. Lacey runs for the door and welcomes in house guest number four. James. This completes our party. The reality of the impending maternal visit darkens my vision.

James Joseph and Lacey May are the youngest of our clan. They had a drastically different experience growing up than the rest of us due to the large age gap. James was always quiet and reserved. Sometimes the look he gave out of the corner of his eye, even as a child, was downright chilling. He rarely had the good graces to blink or break his gaze. This often had me wondering what was going through his twisted little mind.

James was always particular in compulsive kinds of ways. The child who didn't like his vegetables to touch. The boy who brushed his teeth after every meal. The kid who always demanded to know where you were going, what you were doing and what was happening next, like a clingy cruise director. Upsetting his schedule unleashed the little monster within him. He did not like change nor did he take it well when it happened.

A sheepish smile and a tucked in polo shirt are the first things I notice. His hair is pasted down. Part of me instinctively looks for a pocket protector to complete the ensemble. No such luck. The rest of us go around looking like a band of gypsies while he could be a CPA. He looks like our father, down to the same hardness in his eyes. This catches me off guard and sends a chill down my spine. I have to stare up to the ceiling to avoid betraying the thought with my eyes.

We say our polite "hello" and Lacey gets the troops motivated. It's time to go to the hospital for our mother; I am none too thrilled. Silver doesn't have a car. Bobby's looks like it's held together by the power of bumper stickers and positive thinking. Lacey has her Vespa. This leaves James and myself as designated drivers. A look into the street reveals a shiny black cargo van. This could get interesting.

"I can take everyone," James offers quietly. No one really pays him attention. I wait for someone to say no but no one responds. I like to be behind my own wheel, so I guess it's up to me.

"That's okay, I can take my car too. Someone can ride with me if they want. We'll meet up at the hospital?" James looks pinched but complies. Lacey calls shotgun with me, while the other two crawl into the big, dark van.

"Are you sure you don't want to go with the others?" I glance her way.

57

"Oh no, I wouldn't want you to be alone." I can read the half-truths in her voice and in the way she slouches. Curious.

It's not far to the hospital. Going most of the way across this small town is only about fifteen minutes if you hit the lights right, or know the back roads. James takes off for the main drag. I take the scenic route; Lacey and I still have some catching up to do now that we're both awake and sober. I let the noise of the road fill the silence for the first few minutes. Lacey stares out the window, mesmerized by the passing scenery.

"She's never been the same since Dad left."

Skipping the small talk and getting right to the meat. I don't really have much to say on this topic and offer up a halfhearted shrug instead. Lacey continues to stare out the window as she talks.

"It broke her spirit, I think. When he was gone." She pauses, deep in thought. "Do you have any idea how bad it feels to be rejected by a low-life loser?"

-13-

The hospital is just how I remember it. Floor tile, dated with age and too many coats of poorly applied wax, the smell of sickness and institutional disinfectant hanging heavy in the air, yellowed failing lights turning everything to a ghastly sallow hue... it makes my head swim. Everything about this place makes my skin crawl and my stomach want to churn. Happiness never lands you in the hospital. Places like this are charged with negative emotion.

Lacey has a certainty in her step, leading me down the maze of hallways. I keep my eyes down to avoid engaging the sick and the frail staring up at me with helpless desperation and fear. Reaching out with shriveled bruised hands. Crying out with toothless mouths, grabbing at any flicker of life that passes by. Gasping for one last breath of humanity.

Get your own. You can't have mine.

Hushed voices greet us as we turn in to a room, the oversize door barely cracked open. James, Bobby and Silver are already there. So much for the back roads. I avoid looking at the bed for as long as possible. It's easy at first as the other siblings pow-wow about the state of

events. I spend ample time studying the details of the room. Ceiling tiles, floor tiles, window trim, piece of medical equipment and switches on the wall; they all serve to keep me occupied. The group slowly migrates, and I can't feign ignorance for much longer.

The worn blanket is tucked in tightly over her body, almost like a cocoon. It doesn't look comfortable; nothing about this place does. The bed inclines and the pillows leave her head propped up, long faded hair in a rats nest of tangled ponytail beside her face. I can feel a frown on my face, lips drawn tight and tense with apprehension. Looking at the others, I can see I'm not alone.

Lacey tenderly picks her hand up and cups it in her own. The rest of us stay still, arms folded in various positions. It's a marvelous study in body language. After a time there is a slight stir and tired eyes crack open, not really showing any focus. Lacey coos at her but I don't listen; I'm lost in my own world of thoughts.

Hazel. Hazel Jane Shaw, mother to our brood. Lying there she's not far from being a lifeless shell of what once was a bright and tortured woman. She suffered in her life. I almost wished her peace. Peace I knew she would never get, even in death. The hand of my father was a hard one. Lumps and ridges remained on her face, telling tales of the old days, the bad days. She bore enough plates in her face to border on being bionic but things had been stitched together and reconstructed over the years the best they could at the time. Still, the trauma showed through her thinning, ashen skin.

I could see the scar under her hair, tracing ear to temple, from the time I had drank the last of the milk, leaving none for his evening meal. She hadn't known; I hadn't told her. We shared the wrath for not knowing better, for being stupid, selfish cows. I escaped with a black eye. She didn't escape. She should have ended up with twenty stitches, but that wasn't' the type of thing you went to the emergency room for. People would ask questions. *I tripped,* only worked so many times.

Our house always had a full stock of butterfly bandages. They were inexpensive, accessible and mandatory for survival. I remember the swatch of hair she had to cut away to make them stick. Hair pulled back, flesh seamed together, she looked like a brain surgery patient. Sometimes I wondered if that were really the case. After that the hair was always swept forward for disguise, the pain hidden amongst the curls and shadows of ill trimmed bangs. A style most of us shared at one time or another.

A ragged gasp escapes her lips, causing me to jump. Everyone looks at her. Everyone looks at me. She's awake and staring, boring a hole directly in to my forehead.

"What is she doing here?" rasps from her lips. Her eyes are cold, dead like a shark.

Lacey does her peacemaking dance. "Mama, I thought you'd like to see her since you haven't been well. She wanted to come." Her smile beams up at me encouragingly, convincingly. I almost believe it. My shoulders slump but my tongue is tied. I manage a shrug. Suddenly I'm twelve again.

I marvel at how easy it is to be reduced to nothing in the blink of an eye. Nothing matters; not the past, not the present, only the disdain and judgment. It's like falling into a vacuum, the air sucked clean from your lungs. There's no way to gasp, no way to speak. *Why the fuck did I come?*

The breathing echoes in my ear, the sound of the oxygen pushing in and out of her nostrils, the hoarseness of breath emitting from her, even under no physical stress. Misery personified. Finally the exterior matched the interior.

My ears become suddenly aware of faint wisps of

breaking local news droning in the back ground. *A grisly discovery today at a local learning institution...* Oh yeah. That. I manage not to smile. *Fucking meat head.*

Silver starts to regale our mother with fantastical tales of carnie life. At least that's what I call it. She's nothing more than a traveling sideshow skank. Different towns, different names, different lovers every night. She makes bringing culture to the great unwashed sound much more artistic than whorish. I silently wonder what kind of health plan they have and hope it's a good one. Wouldn't want her weeding out the gene pool one lay at a time.

James has little to say. He stands there looking drawn. To see him now he's a near picture of our father, just without the boorish bravado. It gives me chills. Again, I wonder how mother feels about it. She almost died while in birth with James. The doctors had warned her about getting pregnant again; that her body had been weakened from child bearing, abuse and age. The life forms she already tended to were draining her; she didn't need more. But it wasn't up to her, it was never her choice.

Every time she tried to protect herself, he found out. Pills flushed, diaphragms pin-holed, he always found a way to perpetuate his seed. It was easier if she was willing. It was more titillating if she wasn't. She learned not to flinch, not to show the disgust and hatred as he tore at her. That alone was her greatest defense. Play dead. Close your eyes and play dead.

Too many days I found her sobbing in her bed after he left for work. She could hold back the tears, but only for so long. "Mommy's fine... don't worry..." I heard it again and again. As I grew older, pity and concern grew into ambivalence and I learned to quit checking on her. The bloodshot eyes across the breakfast table said it all. Eventually it became her own fault for tolerating it; therefore, she deserved it. I had my own wrath and late night visits to deal with. If she couldn't protect herself, how could she even pretend to be able to protect me?

Every woman for herself.

"Oh, I have an announcement..." Bobby chimes in. Heads swivel as he takes the floor. "I didn't bother telling anyone since it was rather spontaneous, but I got married a while back." Lacey gasps with excitement, Silver pats him on the back, James does what James does best; stands there motionless.

"Who's the lucky lady?" Silver purrs.

"Her name is Crystal. Crystal Graves. We had a nice little commitment ceremony at a local music festival. It was awesome." He can't contain his excitement. This thaws me a little.

"So we have a Mrs. Bobby Shaw in the family," Silver concludes. "Who would have guessed you'd be the first one to go?"

"Actually. . . " Bobby pauses, looking pensive. Now I'm curious.

"Actually, what?" It gets the better of me.

"Well... See... It's just that Crystal doesn't have any brothers, and her parents were both only children. So we thought it would be a nice sentiment if I took her family name instead." He explains it like it's the most common thing in the world.

"Robert Raymond Graves," I'm the first to say it out loud. My mouth works over the foreign words a couple times. "Actually... it has kind of a nice ring to it."

It's really a brilliant move. What better way to get another step away from the family legacy? The others don't seem quite as impressed, the cliché arguments about societal norms abound. It bores me. The conversation devolves from there and that's my cue to leave. I don't say goodbye, I just slip out. No looking back.

-14-

I sit in the car, hands on the wheel, debating my next move. Lacey will be stranded if I leave, and I wasn't done talking to her yet. The others are not my concern. Mother could be dealt with later. I'm not in a hurry, it's not my style.

A full twenty minutes later Lacey finally shows up. I'm bordering on dreamland but I can virtually hear her frown.

"Why did you leave?" The hurt washes over her face.

"Look, kid. It was clear that there was no point in me standing around. I don't like to waste my time."

"But mom asked about you."

"Oh? Well good for her. She looks fine, I'm not sure what all the worry is about." I lie. Lacey's eyes take on a watery glint. Shit. Little sister had cried enough, she didn't need more of it from me.

"Let's just go home. I told them I'd make lasagna. We'll have a nice family dinner." Never have such simple words sound so sad. Her veiled optimism still astounds me. We both know that we won't have a "nice family dinner."

The ride home is solemn. I take the main streets this time, trying to cut down on the expanse of awkward silence. She asks me to stop at the local grocery, which is now a chain. Everything is a chain now. Gone are the days of the mom and pop establishments. Discount cards and fuel perks rule the world.

Fresh bread and a big jar of marinara later, we're standing in the checkout, waiting for our turn like good little sheeple. The people in front of us are catching up on the daily gossip in true small town manner.

Did you hear? Oh my gosh!!... to the jugular? Who would DO something like that?... This world we live in now- a days... Monster! I stand there nonchalantly. People are idiots. Lacey seems to be equally unmoved but I chalk it up to the day's events.

"Did you hear about the Principal?" She finally breaks the silence as we cruise down the drive aisle. "I can't believe that could happen in our old school. And to someone we knew."

"You knew him?"

"Well, sure. It's not that big of a town. I remember him from when you were in school too, I think," she pauses and grins. "Didn't you used to have a crush on him?" I cringe.

"Him? Nah, doesn't sound like me. We didn't exactly run in the same circles, you know." *Eyes forward.* "From what I remember, at least." I didn't run in anyone's circle. The statement was painfully true.

"Hmmm, I could have sworn..." She gets lost in thought against the backdrop of the darkening sky.

"You were young, easy mistake. You know I wasn't allowed to date anyhow, it didn't really matter who I had a crush on." She manages a small nod. The silence returns.

The duplex is already inhabited. Silver has

possession of Lacey's spare key. I can hear Bobby in the other room but I don't see signs of James.

"Where's James?"

"Oh, he said he had to go get something or whatever. Maybe he needed some air or something... whatever," Silver waves her hand dismissively. Gypsy music shrills in the background. I look at her. "That's me on the tin whistle. We're trying to get the demo circulating, maybe go viral." All I can do I nod and roll my eyes when she looks away. Far be it from me to crush her dreams, not that my logic could. Her version of reality was one of purely her own creation. It was far easier to avoid judgment if you weren't living by other's rules.

Seeking space, I wander to the living room. This whole homecoming is about as miserable as I expected. I console myself that now I won't have to do it for another twenty years. Or until someone dies. Whichever comes first. The sound of dishes and Silver prattling on echoes from the kitchen. Bobby pads out of the bathroom in yoga pants and I try not to snicker. He is fully channeling his Zen today, I can tell.

The sun drifts slowly behind the line of rooftops hugging the streets. Before long it's dark and the smell of warm comfort food is wafting through the air. James still isn't back. I envy him. My eyes stare blindly at my surroundings in a soft focus.

"Penny for your thoughts?" Bobby is nudging me. I hadn't even noticed he sat down.

"Oh, nothing." He nods but I can see something in his eyes. "What's on your mind?"

"This is just strange. I haven't seen you in... God... twenty years? It's been that long. How is that even possible?" He seems more amazed than upset.

"People come and go in life, I guess. We do what we need to survive."

He looks soulful for a few moments.

"You know... it didn't get better after you left." I

don't have a reply. "It just meant that there was one less of us for him to pick on. Extra attention for us all." He duplicates my frown.

"Sorry...?" In truth, I'm at a loss; if I had to do it again, I wouldn't do it any different. Just sooner.

"I'm not looking for an apology... I understand why you left. Why you had to. It's the same reason Stephen left. And Silver left. And eventually, I left. I felt so bad for James and Lacey but I had to escape while I could. They never really did."

"What do you mean?"

"Dad walked out on them. But they never expressed the urge to get out before that. Not like us." He looks disturbed for a moment. "It was different for them I guess. I never figured out why."

Soon we're both sunk in to the sofa lost in thought. So many years, so many miles, so many breaks and bruises that would never truly heal. The jingle of a door breaks my trance. James is back.

He comes in bearing brown bags. Liquor store. *Yes*.

"I thought we might like a little refreshment for the evening," he explains quietly. "I wasn't sure what everyone liked so I tried to get a selection." James pulls out three bottles of wine; one red, one white and one pink, a bottle of whiskey and a bottle of vodka. "I figured that should cover it." He almost smiles.

His timing is impeccable. Lacey pulls the steaming meal out of the oven while Silver works on setting the table, making little napkin creatures to garnish our plates. Apparently a stint on a cruise ship had taught her this invaluable life skill. The family working in unison reminds me of old times. Occasionally there were days that weren't all bad.

We settle in for dinner, determined to do some serious damage to the feast laid before us. The breaking of bread seems to put everyone at ease. Of course, so do the bottles of wine. And vodka. And whiskey. For once we sit and talk about the old days, but the good parts of the old days. Stories and memories that don't always end with one of us being bloodied and bruised by the strap, the wooden spoon, the hairbrush. It's nice to reminisce when the topics don't make you want to go hide.

Table cleaned up, dishes done and the better half of the booze consumed, and it's barely eight o'clock. Should I go to bed early in self-defense or risk more quality bonding time? I sure as hell don't feel like sitting at the table the entire night. I look for a delicate way to excuse myself so I can slip out the door for a little more space. Silver beats me to it.

"Well, my darlings, the wine has enabled my passionate spirit. I think I'm going to slip out in to the darkness for a while and see what kind of handsome trouble I can get myself in to." She doesn't pause long enough to collect any companions. With a whisk, she's gone.

I too manage to combat Lacey's disappointed face and succeed in prying myself free from the reunion as well. I give Silver enough time to get ahead of me and strike out on my own.

-15-

The cool air steals my breath as I head out the
door. My legs need to stretch so the car stays parked
tonight. Enough layers to break the wind keep me from
being too uncomfortable in the crisp night. Light frost is
already creeping along the edges of the empty darkness.
Stars shine bright in the clear black sky, despite the glow of
the city lights. It's going to be a cold one on the
gravestones tonight.

Silver is nowhere to be seen. I walk quietly down
the sidewalks, ears perked for noises in the shadows, the
knife in my pocket my only security. Who would possibly
want to give me trouble?

It doesn't take long for me to stumble upon a
local watering hole. Hole being the operative term. It looks
small and warm. I'm ready to take the chill off, if only for a
moment but I'd like to get a little further away from home
base. My feet carry me onward at an increasingly brisk
pace. The beauty of this town is there is rarely a large
distance between churches and bars. It's not much of a
challenge to find an assortment of establishments in a
relatively small radius.

I settle on a small Irish pub, its glowing shamrock

a beacon in the cold chill of night. The odds of finding a decent drink of something other than light beer piss water are in my favor. The place is small and dark and cozily worn from years of use. My standard seat is open at the end of the bar by the far wall. It's like they've been waiting for me.

The bar tender doesn't pay me much mind for a few minutes, but it gives me time to settle in and warm up my freezing fingers while surveying the scene. The standard assortment of local bar flies and wrinkle room singles seem to populate the place. This generally indicates less potential for trouble. I don't mind.

I order a Guinness and take a harder look around the room. The early edition of the late night news program is up on the small screen in the far corner of the room. They're still reporting on the grisly discovery earlier in the day. It seems to be the most exciting thing they've had in these parts since the last big wing eating contest. The words "no suspects" and "no known enemies" are easy enough to make out and I'm glad to hear at least one of those things, despite being highly skeptical of the other. The ache in my jaw is the consequence of my clenched teeth. *Asshole.*

The Guinness tastes like more. My cash supply tells me I'm good for another round or three. The beer flows while I sit quietly and entertain myself watching the crowd filter in and out like an ocean tide. People-watching is its own form of cheap entertainment. Why sit in front of a TV watching "reality" when you can go observe and participate in your own? The difference of intention between words and body language is amazing. In one corner of the room a younger couple banters toe to toe; clearly an early date in the relationship. The man leans in, pretending to be interested in every word tripping out of his date's crimson, satin lips. She doesn't seem to notice the straying gaze into her v-neck as she talks about what I can only imagine to be her cats and how wonderfully whimsical they are.

The drinks keep coming steady to her, though he's slowed down. She doesn't notice him milking the empty bottle he's had since I walked in. Meanwhile her assortment of bar-wear begins to crowd the table. Eventually the shot glasses come out.

Her expression increasingly dulls until it's clear she's going to have one hell of a hangover in the morning. His doesn't. The more dazed she gets, the sharper the glint in his eye. The molars in my mouth cry out a quiet protest at being ground yet again. Why must girls get so drunk and so careless? It's not becoming.

I try to distract myself with other scenes unfolding around the room but the action is quiet over all. The couple in the corner keeps drawing my eye. Her body language all but says defeat, she could fall asleep in the booth right now and not be aware of the coaster stuck to her head 'til morning. He's trying to expedite the settling of the tab while her eyes look like butterflies fluttering against the wind. Before long he pours her out of the booth and into her jacket, guiding her to the door. It looks chivalrous enough but I'm the nosy sort.

It takes longer to mull over my next move than it does to finish my beer. It might be time to stretch my legs again. A search through my pockets yields enough to cover tab and tip; I don't bother asking for the bill. Before long I'm out the door, again listening to the sounds of the street. These ones aren't hard to mistake.

I stroll down the quiet street, in the direction of the closest alley. Dark alleys. So cliché but still such a good place for trash of all types to accumulate. There's always a flickering or burned out security light. Always. I don't know where the universal rule is written for that requirement but it regularly seems to be the case and this town is no exception. I am not disappointed in my hunt.

Two lovers are silhouetted in the moonlight. Only one is enjoying it.

Drunken, protesting moans of the half-conscious float quietly to me in the dark. He shushes her. He soothes her. He gets impatient because she won't shut up. A crack of hand on skin and a whimper rings out. Silence returns.

Sometimes I hate being a good judge of character.

There are two ways this can go down. I can interrupt and give him time to react, defend, run, or do something stupid. Given that he looks to have a good hundred pounds on me this seems like a bad option. Sweet, silent finesse it is.

It doesn't take much for me to slip down the alley unnoticed. There are plenty of shadows and he has his hands more than full with the drunk mess pinned up against the wall. I can see the outline of his fingers on her face accented by the glint of tears in the moonlight. *Fucking brute.*

My knife is cool to the touch from the night air. The feel of steel reassures me. The blade opens with a nearly imperceptible flick. No one notices. It doesn't take much, stealth is on my side. I barely even have to force his head back - he doesn't have time to protest.

A surprised gurgle is all I hear before he drops. The girl goes from quiet sobbing to hysterics. There's no talking reason at this point, I don't even try. I hit her, hard. She goes down like a ton of bricks. I hate to do it, but the black eye is the least painful option in the long run and I don't have time to dally. I'm sure she won't be there long, I can already hear the convergence of voices in the area. A quick wipe of the blade and I'm on my way, back into the shadows. Getting off the streets seems like a good idea but I still take the long way back to Lacey's.

I near the house and see two figures in the street embracing. The glint and sparkling in the murky road reveals Silver in the moonlight. I can hear her jingle from the bangles she wears. The other figure I can't quite make out; all I can pick out in the distance is a cowboy hat.

Hanging back in the shadows, my nostrils burn from breathing in a shallow rhythm so as not to tip off my presence by the cloud of vapor escaping me. Silver demonstrates some of her belly dancing moves, bangles and belt chiming, accentuated by the crisp air and hard surroundings. Again they embrace but this time I see the hesitation in his stance. He manages to free himself from the many tentacled beast that is my sister, leaving her with a kiss on the cheek and a tip of his hat. Soon an old truck pulls away from the house and Silver dances herself inside. I fight the cold to walk around the block one more time before heading back in.

"Oh he's just delicious! So tall and handsome... and those jeans!... " Silver is already spouting off about her conquest to anyone who will listen. Each layer of clothes she pulls off falls in a jangle to the floor. "I'm going to see him tomorrow night. He's not in town for long either," she sighs. "We're like two ships passing in the night... how *noir*."

"What's his name?" Lacey inquires, enraptured by the chance to have some girl talk. This is the first time I see Silver's mouth shut for even a second.

"Um... Alex? Aiden? Allen? Something like that... not that it's important. He won't be around long enough for it to matter." She gives an impish smile and a wink. The glint in her eye is what disturbs me.

The ringing phone cuts off my mouth, open and eager to pass judgment. Saved by the bell. Lacey answers, looking stricken.

"It's mom... she's dead."

-16-

"Tell them I'm sorry. I wasn't enough."

That's all she wrote in a heavy handed scrawl. Even in death she took the cowards' way out. It wasn't the strokes that killed her, the doctor explained. She had saved up enough pain meds and sleep aids to bridge the gap to the darkness on her own. The only explanation he could offer was how the tests just found her system saturated with heavy metals, and how that could have impaired her reasoning. I knew better. I knew she was a coward. Heaven wasn't gaining an angel tonight.

Lacey finalized the arrangements. It would be simple, inexpensive. Cremation and a walk through the woods to scatter the ashes. We were not a family of means. Stephen only offered to send his regrets with flowers.

"Why *fucking* bother," she mutters as she hangs up the phone. Little sister has finally reached her limit. Even Silver can't comfort her. "Don't even try," she snaps. "You don't care either. None of you care..." The tears start to pour down her cheeks. "It wasn't supposed to be like this..." is all she manages to say through her sobs. Silver throws an arm around her in an attempt at comfort. Lacey

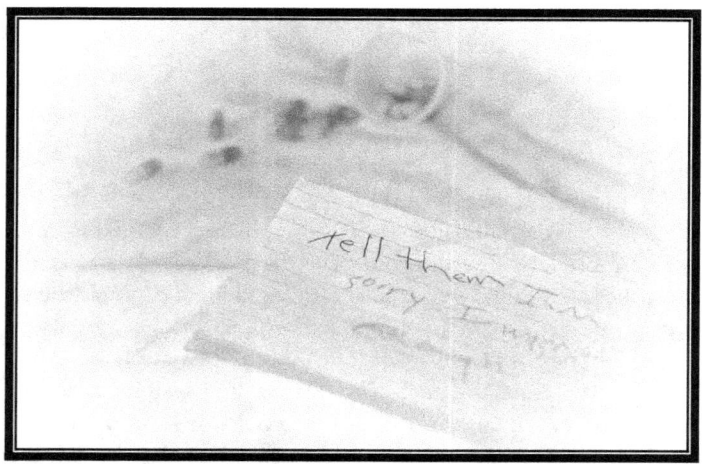

shrugs it off violently.

"Get off me, whore. I don't need you to pretend to care. All you care about is yourself. Have you stopped to listen to anyone else for even a minute since you got here?" Her face glows red with grief and anger. Silver manages to look aghast, like any good actress would.

"Lacey, you're upset, maybe you should..." I hear the words coming out of my mouth. Suddenly I'm the peacemaker.

"Don't YOU start with me too," she growls. "You haven't said a word since you got here. You don't seem upset in the least. After everything we've talked about, where are you? Engrossed in your own little world. You still don't listen. You don't even come in to the same room as the rest of us. You still don't care. You're no better than HER." The boys exchange worried glances but stay on the fringe.

"I... I just can't believe she would do this. She was going to be fine, I made sure of that... it was all fixable. It just doesn't make any sense..." But she's convincing herself, not us.

"Wait... what was fixable?" Bobby chimes in from the corner.

"Her symptoms. They would have reversed themselves soon enough..." Lacey paces, agitated, around the room. Bobby is finally on the move.

"Lacey," he calls her gently, grabbing her by the shoulders. She refuses to look at him; she's just spinning her wheels. "Lacey," he says again more firmly. "Lacey, look at me." Finally he gains a glimmer of acknowledgment. She doesn't speak but her eyes lock on him.

"Lacey, what did you mean about her symptoms? Did you know what was wrong with her?" She just avoids his stare.

"I only wanted to see you all again..." She whispers quietly. "You wouldn't have come otherwise."

The room shows three sets of eyes focused on the unsteady blond, wheels churning and eyebrows furrowed.

"Lacey, look at me again," But her head lolls, almost disoriented. Bobby sits her down in the closest chair. "What was wrong with mom? Did you do something?"

"Just a little," she sniffles. "Only a touch."

"A touch?"

"In the tea at night. She just needed a little to get sick. That's all I wanted. All I needed. It worked fine before..." her words trail off into nothingness.

"What did you put in her tea, dear?" His voice is calm and soothing like talking people down was second nature.

"Just a nip of mercury in the chamomile." She looks up at him with her big, golden brown eyes.

"Where did you get mercury?" He keeps the tone warm and even, prompting her to respond.

"Found some old thermometers up in her attic... no one used them anymore... no one missed them..." Her voice sounds little and lost.

"How much did you give her?

"I don't really know. Just a little at first, a tiny bead in the evening tea. Made sure I always used the same cup, just in case. It didn't really seem to do anything right away but eventually she started having spells."

"Is that when she went in the hospital?"

"No, it took a while to build up I guess... I ran out of thermometers pretty quick so I found a way to acquire some thimerosal. It's a mercury laced antiseptic I used to use at work... It took more than I anticipated to reach toxicity, but no one seemed to miss it." Given her unfocused eyes and ever paling face Lacey appeared to be suffering from some exposure of her own.

"But she overreacted... she screwed it all up. Why would she do that? Why now?" I think we all knew why. We all had our experiences and expectations.

-17-

The service was a somber one. Small and quiet. It didn't take much turnaround time really. No one wanted to turn Lacey in, but none of us knew what to do with her. No one at the hospital really seemed to care once the death was ruled a suicide, they were more concerned about who let her stash all of the pills. We dodged a bullet.

Silver left after the ash scattering to go meet her date. She had managed to postpone previously due to a 'traumatic turn of events.' She had comforting in mind now, and did her best to look sullen for him. "Black is so slimming," is all she said as she slipped out the door.

Eventually the others dispersed and I found myself alone with Lacey. It was time for an intervention. I wasn't looking forward to it.

"Talk to me, kid. What's up?"

She avoids my look yet again. It takes a while for her to start. I stay silent as she forms soundless words with her mouth, unsure what to say first.

"I'm so alone," is all she can muster.

"No, you're not. We're all here for you."

"No, you don't understand. Until you all came back, there was no one. No one but me and Mother. It's

been that way for years now. I can't find a friend, can't find a lover. I'm a grown woman now and I can't manage to get a steady boyfriend. They all run out on me, disappear... just like Daddy did..." The last part gives me chills.

"We don't need to rely on men to be happy."

"No. YOU don't." I wince at the sharpness of her tone. "I *want* companionship. I *want* someone to share my day with. To walk through the flowers with me. Something and someone other than these furry beasts I foster. I... I don't know what happens. I have a date, maybe two. Things seem to be going great and then it's like *poof*, I never see them again," she tries not to sniffle. "Am... Am I that repulsive? That worthless?" The saline trickle begins once again. I frown.

"Silver can go pick up a man in one night. Me? Nothing. I can't get them to talk to me, and when I do, I somehow scare them off just as fast. I just am so tired of being alone..."

A noise from the other room draws my attention. James ducks back behind the doorway. I suspect that I have someone else to deal with later. I give Lacey a hug. It feels foreign to me, to let someone close again. It's not my normal inclination. She sobs quietly on my shoulder, years of abandonment pouring from her core. This isn't going to be an easy fix and I'm not that nurturing type.

She sobs long enough to wear herself out. My shirt stains with her tears. Groggy red eyes look up to me, pleading for acknowledgment. I grab her shawl and tuck it around her shoulder. She gives me a weak smile in return. It takes little convincing to get her to turn in for the night, to rest her pretty head. Morning isn't going to make it better, but sleep can dull the pain for tonight.

It's past dusk now. The house is dark and quiet, conversation having eclipsed the sun before the lights were turned on. I sit for a moment, listening, wondering what the others are up to. I'm not sure I have it in me to have another heart to heart. Or another night out at the bars.

I'm stuck.

I find what's left of the whiskey and pour myself two fingers over ice, content to contemplate the darkness. I hear the shuffling of Bobby and James in the other areas of the apartment and the faint murmur of a TV. Light is now spilling under the door that separates us, casting an ambient glow into my cocoon of darkness. I feel violated.

-18-

In truth, I don't know James well. I wasn't really there. I feel a little bit of guilt for that, being the oldest sibling and all. James came along at a time when chaos and survival ruled my life. Mother was desperate to please our asshole father and keep him distracted with another new toy. He liked things that screamed easy, us older ones were getting too difficult to get a rise out of. Not that it stopped him from trying. He liked being able to lay a single finger on a baby or small child and have it go stiff with fear. He got off on intimidating the weak. The power got him hot. Just another form of fucking cowardice. If you cried, if got worse. If you fought, it got worse. If you did not react, it was a challenge. There was no winning. He wasn't happy till you cracked.

Something changed by the time James came around. On a basic level, at least. Maybe he lost his edge, his energy, I don't know. Maybe there were finally enough options that he didn't focus as hard on any single one of us. Maybe he just wanted one of us to grow in his own image, to carry on the tradition. The rest of us, we resisted, we fought, we cowered when we had to and ran when we could.

Stephen was the first male born. He and father were like hot oil and water. Stephen often made him so enraged that the man nearly frothed at the mouth, face red from screaming respect in to him. He was no heir. No prodigy.

Bobby was mild natured; he took after our mother really. Subservient. He was always a little too soft, too delicate to evoke the testosterone-induced ire the same way. He still got his fair share -- of course -- we all did, but he wasn't an alpha. He wasn't a superior challenge; he was too easy to break.

James was different, even as a baby. He didn't react with the same fear the rest of us did. If anything it could be called studious observation. Mimicking my father's moves, even as a toddler, garnered a glint in his eye that I had never seen before. Pride. Father crafted him in his own image. James lacked the vibrato to make you quake in your shoes, but the eyes had the darkness deep inside them. For one so young, getting caught in his gaze was chilling.

He made a habit of quietly informing our father when we tried to get away with things. Where we hid, what we said when we thought no one was around to hear. He was a little narc. The more he informed, the closer the bond became. It didn't take long before we all hated him. Even as a child we couldn't trust him. Little bastard of His Asshole's Secret Service.

Then Lacey came along. Daddy had himself a brand new baby girl. A fresh toy to torture. The next apple of his eye. The old man was back in form, only this time he had a protégé. Despite his involvement, James had a protective streak when it came to Lacey. We slowly began to see how he was running interference between her and the old man. It didn't make things any better on the rest of us but at least Lacey had a shot. She wasn't old enough to see what the rest of us went through. She was too young to understand the stories and before she could I had my four wheels on the road out of there.

Stephen was hot on my heels. In fact, he followed right in my footsteps; dropping out of high school early to get a GED. He got bloodied up by the old man one time too many, taking a chunk or two with him in the process. School wasn't worth spending any more time under the institutional roof than necessary. It was boring. It was political. It was cruel. And that was just the staff.

Ask me about bullies. People have no concept of bullies. The things that happened to me at the hands of my learning institution are still the things that keep me awake at night and lurk in the shadow of the fields and the stadiums. I know they still happen -- to the weak, the sullen, the people who the predators think won't stand up for themselves. The universal victims that no one would ever believe even if they did speak up. Losers. Freaks. Take your pick, the names all meant they wouldn't believe me. I knew that. I didn't even try. There were no *after school special* quality counselors waiting to help the broken. They didn't exist in my world. They waited till you were gone and laughed along with their favorite pupils.

We were both graduates by the time we were sixteen. The brilliant malcontents. Too smart for our own good. Too disenchanted to care. Pain was an easy source of entertainment for those without innocence. An easy way to control how we felt; a cathartic release.

Stephen did the stuff dumb boys do. Fire. Drugs. Stupid stunts for attention. Putting his life at risk for a shot of adrenaline or a petty bet. I wasn't so eager to share; I lacked a taste for the theatrical. A flask and a razor blade were my constant companions. It didn't matter what was in the flask, as long as it was full. I was flexible. The pack of razor blades, kept close to my skin, were my security for when the darkness breathed. I couldn't control what others did to me but I could control what I did to others. A tally of escapes lined my arms and thighs. Every now and then a blond bobble head would turn me in for being suicidal. Dumb bitch. It wasn't that at all. Those weren't the tendencies I was trying to curb.

Silver wasn't quite so focused in her escapism. She just plain dropped out and ran, earning her money playing on street corners during the day and working them when she had to at night. Slowly she worked her way across the country though the fields of gold to the sandy shores of temperate weather. It's much better to be a street performer on the beach rather than in the snow-filled parking lots of home.

The vagabond lifestyle took to her. Countless cities, gigs, lovers; a constant buffet of stimulation. Be whoever you want to be with a simple change of venue. Exotic, demure, it didn't matter. There were even rumors that she passed herself off as a Russian princess for an entire year. Of course, there was knife throwing involved. My family did have an affinity for the blades. Sharp wit and hand eye coordination were a potentially lethal combination.

-19-

Hours pass, much to my chagrin. I wake with a start, to the clatter of bracelets and the glare of an overhead light. My eyes squint to the door, anger on my tongue. Silver trips in over her own feet, giggling and clearly intoxicated. She's not alone. Someone tall and thin follows her, someone in a cowboy hat. Silver shushes him drunkenly, making more noise than she would speaking in a normal voice.

I lean back in the chair and wait for them to stop fooling around long enough to realize they're not alone; it takes more time than it should. She won't take a step forward because she's too busy feeling up her new friend. He politely dodges most of the advances, but loses a few battles to the great war of getting her past the foyer.

A forward nudge and they both come spilling in, almost landing at my feet. Silver giggles as the strangers gray eyes shoot up to meet mine. Only then do I recognize the ten gallon hat. Shit.

My pupils shine like saucers and my breathing stops as I watch him watching me, both calculating the next move. There is no denying the recognition but Silver doesn't notice - she's enjoying the tumble. He straightens up and gets her off the ground, suddenly very stiff around his new found company.

"Ooooooh Anna, we didn't see you there. What's up, buttercup?..." She's slurring. It's not cute. "Anna, I want you to meet..." Insert drunken pause. "I wannnnt you to meet... um... " Serious look of concentration. "I want you to meet..."

"Alan," he tips his hat, trying not to be obvious. I pause for a moment, thoughts racing.

"Nice to meet you... Alan." I do let a small smirk slip between my lips. Only he sees.

"Alan! Yes, Alan. He's the most *wonderful* dancer! We were out all night, there was this band, and a bull and a... " she drones on and on. Neither one of us pays attention. I don't even need to nod as she keeps going regardless.

Curiosity as to how this plays out is overshadowed by the sneaking suspicion that I won't like the results. My spidey senses, they tingle, and despite the painted on Levi's it's not a good tingle. There are no such things as coincidences in my world. If you think things are that serendipitous or that whimsical, you don't have a clue.

"So... Alan? Is it?" My teeth flash in an attempt to smile. "How did you two kids meet?" I can feel my eyebrow quirking and the smirk plastered to my face.

"Uh,well, I was at the bar and this little lady came up and introduced herself." He manages to look slightly embarrassed.

"Did she now?" My voice directs to Silver.

"Well of course, darling," she drapes an arm over him, flaunting her find. "Wouldn't you want to introduce yourself? I mean, I assume we still bat for the same team, don't we? Or has that changed? I lose track." Claws out. Bitch.

"I would say yes, but I'm not sure which team you're on at any given moment. Wouldn't want to compromise myself." The daggered smile is served and volleyed.

"Some people are so *square*," she purrs, tugging on his collar. I resist the urge to put my square peg through her round hole. "Alan, dear. I'm going to go freshen up a bit, powder my nose and all that. I'll be right back." She trails her fingers down his arm as she backs away, lecherous gaze in her eyes.

At last she is out of earshot. My turn.

"Mind telling me what the *hell* you're doing here?" If I were a cat, my tail would be flicking. The tone hissing through my lips is neither jovial nor amused.

"It's an amazing coincidence," he starts. Involuntarily my eyes roll back in my head, with a snort.

"Try. Again."

His face grows dark, more serious. He's sizing me up, debating his next play.

"Well I must say it is *somewhat* of a coincidence. I hadn't planned to see you here."

"See me where, exactly?"

"In this town, of course. What are the odds...?" he trails off. He's not trying to sell it very hard; I'm not sure if I should take that as a compliment or an insult.

Saved by the clang, Silver trips back in the room, cutting my inquisition short. She's slightly more put together and definitely more graceful. Damn her.

"Anna, would you be a dear and give us a little privacy to have our *night cap*? I wasn't quite done getting to know Alan as well as I had wanted to..." She gives a bawdy smile. She's beyond being coy.

"Sure, no problem," I hesitate, still trying to decipher the situation. "You kids have a good night." I turn and walk away. I don't look back.

-20-

I dream in color. Vivid strokes of the subconscious blurring my thoughts. The events of the day and the memories dredged up over the visit mingle and fester in my brain. Even in sleep there is no escape. The tears, the pain, they all come rushing back. The dark room, the profile of my father back lit by the hall light. The allium and bourbon soaked whispers in my ear. *"You're my favorite. You'll always be my favorite... daddy's... little... girl..."* The cold night air hits my body as the covers lift. My teeth clench both to control the shiver and the noises of protest.

He comes for me, hot and sadistic, as he always does. I wait. I wait till he gets close. Just a little closer, closer, close enough... I lash out and I strike, hands turn into claws. I rake him and shred at his face and his eyes, any bit of flesh I can get my fingers in to. He screams in fury and then in pain, thrashing around, grabbing for the beast he can no longer see. I shred and I scream and I curse him and everything he's done to me and my family. I shred him until he's nothing more than a twitching pile of hamburger and entrails. But the catharsis doesn't stop, I don't stop screaming, I don't stop making up for all the years, all the wasted time, I don't stop...

"ANNA!"

Something is shaking me, grabbing at me. I lash out, catching the offender square in the jaw. Bobby lets out a surprised yelp and leaps back, covering his now swelling lip. He looks stricken. It takes a minute for my consciousness to revive, stitching together the current time and place.

"Oh Bobby, I'm so sorry, I didn't mean to..." My hand is over my mouth, choking off the words. I'm mortified.

"Anna, are you okay?" He looks genuinely concerned about my well-being. "You were screaming in your sleep. And thrashing something fierce," he tacks on with a small smile, rubbing his sore jaw.

I shake my head like an etch-a-sketch, trying to rattle the cob-webs clear and regain clarity. I feel disoriented. Disjointed. Ashamed. I'm at a loss. I look around to see who else is enjoying the freak show but we appear to be alone. I run my hands through my hair and feel the cold sweat along my hair line. I pretend not to notice and look at him solemnly.

"Tell me what happened after I left home."

The flicker in his eyes sets the scene more than a thousand words ever could.

"I'm not sure exactly what you want to know." He stares at the floor absently. "If you're asking if he made life worse for us after you left... Yes. He did. He did not take kindly to being defied. To be made a fool of. That shouldn't be a surprise." His eyes study me.

"What happened to make him leave?" I don't feel like beating around the bush in the wee hours. Bobby's forehead wrinkles for a moment. It's not a look of anger so much as a look of confusion.

"To be honest... I'm not exactly sure. One day he was there, being his usual self. The next day, he just didn't come back. No note, no warning, no indication. Just... gone. After all of that. After *everything*. Gone." He spits out the words like bitter pills.

"I can't believe he just split like that. Even for him it sounds like a dumb move." I knew the premise of the leaving, I just could never quite wrap my head around it.

"The worst part was mom... for as much as she loathed that man, she was devastated. She should have been rejoicing."

"It was all she knew. She based her value on his whims. Less bruises meant more love. The illusion of acceptance kept the cycle churning."

"She didn't know how to go back in to the real world. How to work. How to act. How to be anything but an abused house wife. He left and she had no one to talk to. No friends, no family.. All of them had been alienated years ago. He didn't even let her go to the funeral when Grandma died. He said we couldn't afford the gas. I think he didn't want to be stuck being responsible and watching us. Either way, he was an ass." He pauses, lost in thought. "I was glad when he was gone. I didn't think twice about that. I felt bad for not feeling worse."

"I felt horrible for leaving you all behind to suffer. I'd have taken you with me if I could, but I was only sixteen. I barely was able to fend for myself." The tell-tale lump builds in my throat, but I manage to swallow it hard. That man won't make me cry ever again. I swore that the day I left. The bile rising at the thought of him pushes back the looming tears. Works every time.

The sandman tugs at me again. I don't want to return to my prison of dreams but the body needs to rest. This seems to be a reoccurring theme in my life. Push it to the breaking point, then push it a little more. Bobby sees my focus wavering; I can tell because I see it in his face too. The sandman is calling us both back.

I grab my blanket and we sit together on the floor, against the couch, lightly bantering and drifting in and out of consciousness.

-21-

Sunlight breaks through the window. I awake still propped up, head resting on Bobby's bony shoulder. He's still breathing softly, stuck in the throes of slumber. My neck vertebrae strongly protest my attempt to look around the room, it's a wonder I can move my head at all. Age is taking its toll. It always happens sooner than you think.

I grimace and listen for sounds of the kitchen. All seems quiet yet I can't get back to sleep so I make a date with the coffee maker. The blankets I leave snugged up around Bobby so he doesn't catch a chill. I return to my previous station from the night before. There is jewelry all over the table, which can only be Silver's. Bracelets of the bangle variety, chandelier earrings and little silver star pins pepper the worn plastic table cloth. I shove them neatly into a pile and go about my business. Silver breezes in and out of rooms as casually as a hurricane. There are parts and pieces of her everywhere, in a state of constant chaos. Trying to ignore her won't work. One way or another you are forced to acknowledge her presences, even if it is just to work around it.

The final gurgle of the coffee maker makes me twitch. It's too early to be edgy. Still in a haze, I go through the motions of morning java preparation, not paying mind to what I'm doing. My hands, no more awake than the rest of my body, let my newly filled cup of boiling hotness slip clumsily through, crashing into the counter and sending shards of ceramic and molten beverage flying. *Mother f-...* I curse at myself, mostly under my breath, and scramble for the nearest piece of fabric to sop up the mess.

"I don't think you want to do that."

Startled, I jump and curse myself yet again. There's the cowboy but for once his hat is in his hands, not perched neatly on top of his shiny brown hair. I curse myself twice as hard.

"What's wrong with my approach?" I snap, harsher than I intend to.

"Well, for starter," he takes a step towards me and the mess. "That's your sister's scarf." A faint smile crosses his lips. I swear I see his eyes glint.

A sidelong glance into my hands reveals the truth in his words. *Damn it,* again.

"So it is..." My eyes stare at it blankly, pretending to take notice while my hands resist all urges to plunge it into the pool of seeping liquids. He leans in to pick up a towel lurking daringly close to my elbow. The tiny hairs on the back of my neck bristle and mock my attempt to remain unaffected. "What are you doing?" my voice chokes out in a hoarse whisper. He hovers, close to my face, taking a moment longer than he should.

"Cleaning up your mess." The tone makes me shiver. It's not a good shiver.

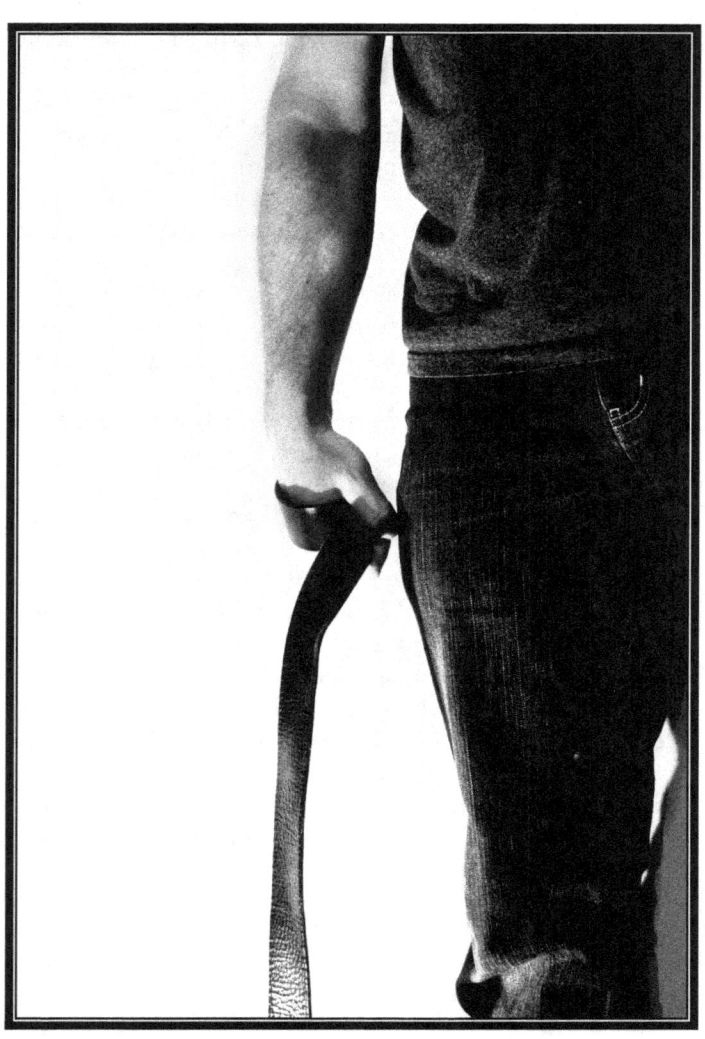

-22-

Bobby pads in to the kitchen, rubbing his neck, only navigating through one eye as he adapts to the light. We exchange the morning pleasantries and he helps himself to the brew.

"Did I miss anything?" He looks around the empty room and gives me a lop-sided grin.

"Nope. Not a thing." I blow on my coffee and take another sip. The hot shower is calling, promising to work the knots out of my shoulders and back. If I don't get in there soon it's going to get worse before it gets better. I finish up and leave Bobby to the quiet.

The hot water scalds my skin but I lean in to it, letting the searing drops pelt the sins of the past off my body. The effect never lasts, but it does feel good for a fleeting moment. Currents run down over my arms, running the tracks of the scars like tortured tributaries carved into the land from years of pressure and erosion. I trace them with my fingers, feeling the sensation shift from steaming red flesh to pale, nerveless tissue.

My ears strain occasionally, listening for other activity in the house, but there is none to pick up. Apparently I'm the early riser and I'm just fine with the nice chunk of time it provides. By the time I am out, Bobby is back on the couch, curled up like a child under the blanket that's pulled up to his eyebrows. Silver and Lacey are still sleeping it off in their respective corners. James slumbers quietly in his sleeping bag. Best not to disturb the nest.

I finish up and grab my bag to go chuck in the car. It's feeling like a quick getaway kind of day. At least it's nice to know you have the option and are prepared for what the day might throw at you. It won't be long before I've overstayed my welcome.

The morning air is cool against my freshly scalded skin. It only feels good for a moment before the chill consumes me. My cheeks feel raw in the stiff wind, forcing me to tuck my head down inside the neck of my shirt. I survey the morning activity up and down the street. It's a weekday now, a bright and shiny Monday morning. Another week to work your ass off for another weekend, and then do it all over again. The neighborhood rises and falls in waves of commuters. Traffic ebbs and flows in the streets and intersections. The closer it gets to starting time, the more horns you hear blaring in the distance. People are late, people are hurried, people are pissed off. Yes, that sounds like a Monday. I sit in my car to escape the frigid breeze and enjoy the show.

Before long, round two of the commuters emerge. Students, housewives, service technicians. Trucks rumble by on their way to businesses or random warehouses throughout the city. Drop off, restock, drop off, restock; round and round they go. The soccer moms kill me. Almost literally a couple of times. Seems that a parked car is no threat to a baby Hummer and a cell phone. They whisk off to their parent/teacher conferences, grocery stores, nail appointments. The number of velour sweat-suits with heels makes me ashamed on behalf of sensible women everywhere. My nose wrinkles in disgust, but it's early yet; there's always something more to see.

A tap on the window sends me diving for my bag and back up knife. Easier to reach than a pocket at this point. My composure returns before making a total ass of myself. James gives me that creepy, dead eyed smile that only James can do so well. He motions to the passenger door, and I wave him in. It takes a moment to shake off the cold before conversation even is an option.

"So what are we looking at?" He scans the activity on the street around us. I'm still not used to his voice as an adult. It's foreign to me. I recognize the dialect, the tone, but it's both familiar and yet alien all at the same time. I look out on the street and shrug.

"Just taking in the scenery, I guess. Didn't want to risk waking anyone up. They need their sleep."

James nods in acknowledgment.

"Same here. Bobby said I have you to thank for the coffee. It was nice to wake up to."

"Yeah, that was me. Sorry there wasn't more left. I didn't realize we all relied so heavily on the caffeine crutch." I actually catch myself smiling at the notion. Sometimes we're more alike than I'd like to think. Sometimes that concerns me.

James glances towards my bag. "Are you leaving already?" There's a pout to his lip that catches me off guard. I shift uneasily.

"Maybe. We'll see. I'm not sure, really. I don't want to be a burr in the saddle. After yesterday with Lacey, I don't really know if I should stay around any longer... make things worse." His body straightens at the mention of her name. "I don't think she's going to get what she's looking for out of us... out of me." His lips look thin and tight.

"I don't know. I don't really know what you have to offer us." His tone is neutral enough I don't bother to bristle. "You're another one who abandoned us as soon as you possibly could. Four of you walked out on us. Personally, I don't see the point of trying to get to know you now. We all have our separate lives."

Touché.

I'm dealing with years of anger. Years of anger are seething under all of our skins, it just manifests in different forms. We've all had our crosses to bear. We all have different scars. Some heal but haunt us with the constant reminder. We carry a piece of our lives with us, burned in our skin, in our minds. I wish it was one or the other, but it's both. It's always both. The pain, it works to the surface, even if that's not where it started. Like a splinter, festering under the skin until finally the body rejects it and starts to push it out obtrusively in tattered flesh and pockets of pus.

The emotions bubble up in the same regard. One way or another, they're working their way out and it won't go without notice. It can't stay concealed inside forever. They have their way of coming out at the least desirable times. Moments of weakness, moments of fear, moments of frustration and anger. Our defenses down, we lash out and we slip. Some of us slip more than others. Some of us can't stop slipping.

I don't know what to say to James. I can't fault him for his sentiments, as much as I'd like to. How was I to know I would start the exodus? Survival was the name of the game. It's been the name of my game since I was old enough to remember. The stakes may change, the geography morphs, but it always comes down to survival. Fight or flight. One lesson that enraptured me during our lousy excuse for a psychology class.

When pushed to the edge, the human condition can be unpredictable. A person, normally reserved and shy, may face up to the bully, the tormentor, the demon in their head, and stare them down toe to toe. In contrast, the big, the bold, the brash... if you give them a taste of their own medicine, don't cower, don't flinch... you'll likely find out what color of yellow they really are. It's all bluster, at least most of the time. And those are the odds I find myself facing more often than I'd like. Fight or flight, Anna. Fight or flight.

I choose Option C. I disengage his attempt at baiting by not acknowledging that it evokes an emotional reaction in me. Perry, thrust, counter. Maybe it really is fighting after all, the evasive maneuvers. We haven't sized each other up yet, truly. Not completely.

"Well James, you're right to a degree. We left. You got left a lot of times. But I only left you once, I can't be responsible for the others. I can't do the penance for our father. Lord knows I would have thanked my lucky stars for that bastard to be found dead in a ditch somewhere."

Mayhaps I've overplayed my hand. He just eyes me. I see his hand play with the surface of the door handle, but his eyes don't move. They don't blink. They just look through me. I manage to thwart the chill I feel building at the base of my spine. He is but a grasshopper. He has no idea who I am; what I've seen, what I've been through, what I've done. He shouldn't be so flippant, it is unwise. I don't take well to intimidation. All of those things still don't tell me why I feel so uneasy around him.

"He wasn't that bad. You're such a sensationalist," he snarks. The words hit me like an open palm to the face.

"Are you fucking kidding me? Seriously, James, please tell me that you're joking."

"No, I'm not joking. I heard about all the stunts you used to pull. All the crap you dragged home and got in trouble for. It's no wonder he gave you hell, clearly you deserved it."

Aghast. Jaw to the floor, stunned. I feel my head reel. My face flushes hot and my hands go cold. I point a finger so far in to his face he has to back up against the door of the car. All I can manage is a growl through gritted teeth, jaw clenching as I speak.

"You. Have. No. *Right*. If that's what you think of me, of us. You have no idea what really happened in that house. You were spared and fed propaganda by the pig-headed ass. Somehow the Universe took care of the problem early for you. I would love to know how the hell that is fair, but you know what? It doesn't matter. I did my time. I suffered. I took the lashes from the belt. I took the pelting from any inanimate object within hands reach. The slaps, the punches, the arms broken from twisting. I got so good at setting my own fingers they didn't even bother taking me to the doctor anymore." I cut myself off and lean back in my seat. The saliva pools around the corners of my mouth, frothy with anger. Just like him.

James' eyes are showing whites, focused on me. He evoked a response, but not the one he was looking for. His face fades to a shade of gray.

"I don't want to talk about it anymore," is all he manages to mumble, hands up in a posture of submission. He won't look at me now. "I'm sorry I came out. I'm going back inside," he fumbles with the door.

"I'm not done talking to you yet." It takes all I have to not grab him by the scruff of the neck. My tone is enough to freeze him. He slumps back in the seat, a willing captive.

I slide up the arms of my jacket, revealing the flesh I tried to keep concealed under normal circumstances. I loosen up the neck too, and start tracing the lines and knots that made up the patchwork of my skin. His eyes follow my hands as they cover each location.

"You see these? All of these? These are from me being a *sensationalist.*" I go over each lump, wincing with the memory of each injury or near miss. "This here," I pointed to a curve in my ring finger. "This is from when I was four, and we were out at the store, and I reached for a candy bar I wasn't allowed to have." He watches.

"This," I trace the bridge of my nose. "This is from the last time he broke my nose. My grades weren't up to snuff and when he saw my report card he slapped me so hard, I stumbled and fell face first into the dining room table. There was blood everywhere. It was almost time for dinner. Mother had a hell of a time keeping everyone out of the kitchen while she shoved gauze up my nose, cleaned the table and still managed to keep dinner on the table on time. He made it clear that if dinner was late, she'd be joining me at the emergency room."

I take the time. I'm explicit with my descriptions, the visions, the memories. Every inch of skin has a story to tell. He grimaces, flinches but is wise enough to keep his mouth shut. I reach for the ankle of my jeans and his hands fly up.

"I'm sorry, I'm so sorry. I get it. I don't' want to see anymore!" He looks like he's going to be sick, eyes like liquid pools of lament. The crack in his voice evokes sincerity. I almost feel sorry. Almost. But I don't.

"I'm done with this. Let's go back inside, it's cold out here." I don't' look at him, I just get out of the car and slam the door. Poor Bessie bears the brunt of his mistake. He pauses a second, unsure, but follows suit. I'm to the duplex door before I even hear my car door slam behind me. It's not worth looking back. Adrenaline is up and I feel loaded for bear. This is what it feels like when you're looking for a fight. I pause at the steps and take a moment to remind myself that I'm among my own kin. They may not be my friends, fact is they're hardly even acquaintances, but they are my family. It's not time to take my bad day out on the others. I muse over the proportional strength of blood verses water. The house door closes quietly behind me and I continue my path up the stairs, still not looking back in acknowledgment.

Rounding the corner at the top of the stairs full

speed, I find myself nose to nose with Silver. This. Is. Not. What. I. Need. She senses the wordless snarl in my breath and for once shies out of the way. Maybe she isn't as dumb as she looks.

The mood inside seems agitated and just plan 'off,' but I can't tell if I'm just projecting at this point. I stick to the edge of the stairwell, trying not to engage in any fresh banter until my blood cools. Looks and glances fly between Silver and Bobby. James is still sulking. I am still ignoring him. A look, a nod, a motion. It's not subtle and it's getting old.

"What the hell is going on?" Bobby and Silver stare me down. Silently, Bobby slides the morning paper in front of my nose. Eyes scan the front page, looking for the punch line.

"Second man found dead, eyewitness places unidentified female at the scene." The suspect sketch is included.

Ah, shit.

Feet to the fire. That's how I feel right now. I feign ignorance, coincidence. Don't let them see you twitch. It's not that hard really, I've kept my cool before, many, many times. I learned that before I even left home. Honestly, I don't bother counting any more. It's just too difficult, too time consuming; it's not about the numbers.

If someone were to ask "How many?" My answer would be "Never enough." The water never runs clean.

Call me a vigilante if you want. It's not quite that noble, nor did I ever try to be. Survival is rarely noble, rarely so cut and dried. It's dirty, primal and base and there are many shades of gray that surround me. I've learned to navigate the subtleties to my own satisfactory rationalization. It's when other people come drifting in to them that things get sticky. Gray to one is black to another, and charcoal to someone else. It's best not to defend your own perceptions of the shades, it only muddies them more or makes you question yourself.

Now I need an exit plan. I'm thankful the family business seems to be wrapping up and James already knows I have one foot out the door. After our little heart to heart it shouldn't be a grand surprise. Unfortunately, I can't say the same for Lacey. She hasn't rousted from her slumber yet and I don't really want to see the questions in her eyes, the hurt as I drive away yet again. Her grand intention to bring the family back together has marvelously backfired. Now we must admit what we've always suspected.

We're worse as a family than we are as strangers. We are the broken.

Darkness, it follows me. It can't be helped. For me it is too late, it was always too late. For them, they have time. They have the grace of youth, they can still seek salvation. I don't care to be saved and I don't need to be forgiven.

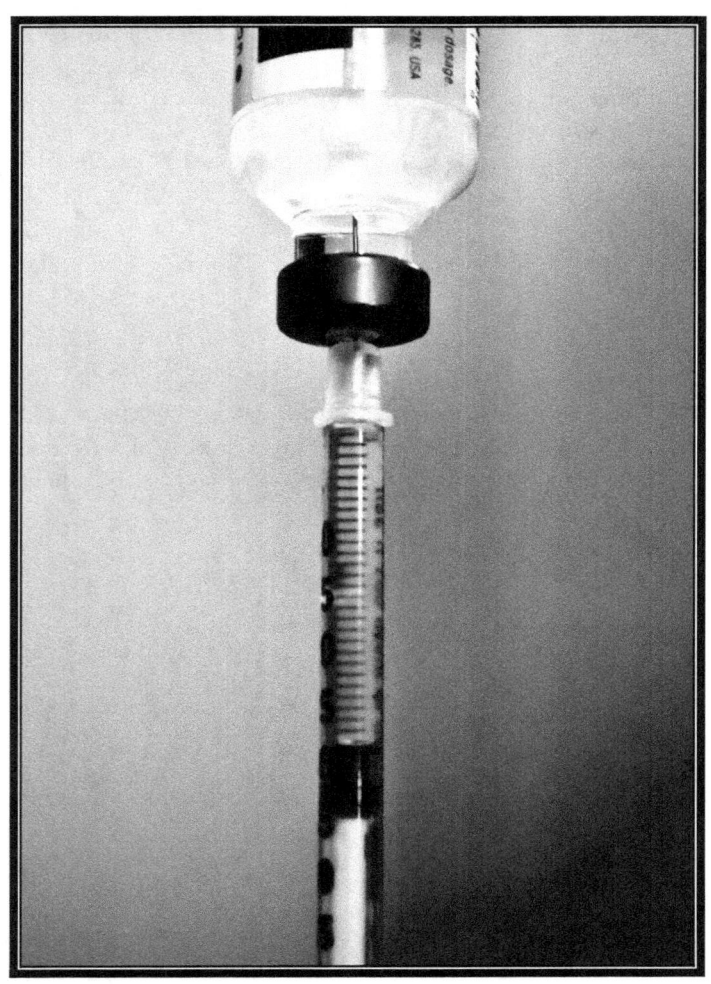

-23-

The poor excuse for a doorbell chimes. It takes a few times before we all pause, straining our ears, to register what exactly we're hearing. Silver's head snaps around to look at the kitchen clock.

"Oh, crap! It's Alan! Stall him for me!" She scrambles to her feet and runs for the bathroom.

I cast a look at the others; none of them are moving. Looks like it's up to me to be the welcoming committee. I pad back down the stairs, wondering what more surprises could possibly await on this lovely fall morning. He sees me coming, through the window. I swear I see a smile on his face.

"Well, good morning again," he grins at me, tipping the hat. Stupid sparkling eyes. I do my best not to glower at him.

"Silver's putting her face on. I wonder which one it will be today," I mutter under my breath. I see the flash of confusion across his face. "Never mind, come on in. She'll be ready in a minute."

Apparently it only takes ninety seconds to clear out of the kitchen without a trace. Back up the stairs and no one is around. Figures. We're all feeling unsociable this morning it seems.

"Coffee?" I already have the mug in my hand. This must be the third pot this morning because it looks entirely too full.

"Sure, sounds good. Black is fine. Just try to keep it in the cup." I shrug and shove it at him. As much as I'd love to go hide as well, I'm stuck entertaining until Silver gets her act together. Given the amount of stage makeup she cakes on, it could be a while. I get comfortable. Had I a tail, I would flick it with bemusement.

Silent sipping of coffee is the only thing that counters the click of the second hand on the clock above. Click. Sip. Click. Slurp. Click. Tap. I watch him, eyebrows arched, waiting for him to do something amusing for me. It's a standoff. I see his eyes lock on the folded newsprint.

"Oh is that the paper? Can I see it?" His hand reaches out before the request fully leaves his lips but I'm still a step ahead of him.

"Oh, sorry, that's not today's. It's old news." I shove it lightly out of the reach of his fingertips. His hand hesitates.

"Oh, okay... never mind..." Another thoughtful sip is sucked through the full lips that I wish I could quit watching. His eyes glance around the room, searching for a topic to fill the silence. He sees the pile of Silver's jewelry on the table, pulling out one of the small stars and tracing it with his fingers. "This is pretty. I noticed your sister likes to wear a hand full of these." His thumb rolls over it thoughtfully.

"You would probably know better than me. I never pay much attention to her costumes." My give-a-shit is broken this morning.

The house is quiet, no one is within earshot. My moxie is peaked after a morning of adrenaline spikes. I catch myself tapping my foot against the table leg, trying to release some of the excess energy. I look at him, leaning in. He smiles sweetly. I swear it's his default move.

"So... Alan," I purr. I have his interest in a heartbeat. "You mind telling me, 'cause I'm curious... what you're really doing here?"

"Having coffee?" he answers blankly. It makes me

frown.

"Try again."

"Well, I'm here because your sister invited me." His tone is even, careful.

"Third time's the charm." My eyes narrow slightly.

"I'm... I'm not quite sure what you mean," he lies to buy time.

"Please tell me it's all a great coincidence. Go ahead, try it." He doesn't have an answer on the tip of his tongue this time.

"No use blowing smoke up your ass, is it?" The change in tone grabs my attention. Somehow I can't help but smile.

"Not generally. It takes at least three dates for that." I pause. "Spill it."

A long look around the room, checking for ears and the thinness of walls makes him lean in to speak in confidence.

"I'm going to say this and I'm going to say this *once*. Only because I don't want you or your family to get hurt." He surveys the room again to buy some time but I can see the wheels turning in his head. "Your sister is a *person of interest.*" His voice drops so low I can barely believe I heard him right.

"What?!" My whisper is quiet but sharp, hands clenched tighter around my coffee mug.

"Look, I'm not going to get in to the details but we've been tracking her for a long time. There's been a series of deaths connected to the shows she travels with. Took a while to see the pattern but the investigation led us here."

"Shut the fuck up." It's more of a statement than a command. I shake my head in disbelief. This makes things infinitely more interesting.

"I know it's hard to imagine, that someone could

do something like that."

I nod sagely, wide eyed. I don't smile no matter how much I want to.

"There have been a couple incidents around town here too, since you guys all came back. Not her usual pattern, but she's not with her normal safety net either. We're looking in to it."

Fabulous.

"So, explain to me how exactly we ended up crossing paths? Were you tracking me to get to her?"

"Oh no, nothing like that! Actually, that *was* a bit of a coincidence. Her caravan was last seen out in the direction you were coming from. I was just picking up the trail when I saw a damsel in distress." He flashes that million dollar smile. I am immune.

"Well this is a fine bit of business, isn't it..." I toy with my cup, thinking over the ramifications of this revelation.

"Listen Anna, this is serious. You can't say a word. You may be in danger if she suspects any of you know something."

Somehow, I don't agree, but I play along. It may be easier to burn this bridge than I thought.

"I wouldn't dare say anything. Clearly, if this is true, she needs help that we can't provide. It's for the best if she's apprehended." I worry that I'm a bit too cooperative, but there isn't time to care. The bathroom door pops open as my voice stops.

Silver comes swirling out of the bathroom, a vision in emerald fringe and glinting costume jewelry.

"A bit much for a weekday morning, don't you think?" I don't bother concealing the snark in my voice.

"Oh Anna, deeeeeear Anna. One thing you'll learn in life... maybe... is that any time is a good time to dress up. You don't need an *occasion*." Yes, she uses air quotes. I briefly entertain a vision in my head of slapping her. It makes me smile. I bat my eyelashes at her innocently, smirk not hidden on my face. It makes her frown. This makes me even happier.

"Well dear, we must run along. One last daylight tour of the city before I must bid you adieu. Parting is such sweet sorrow." She traces her fingers around Alan's collar. He has the good grace to blush but the obvious discomfort only drives her affections. It's power.

Within seconds he's up on his feet, and with a nod heads towards the door with her jingling behind him. I watch them go, offering up a little salute when he looks back. The last thing I see is his frown as it disappears down the stairs.

My stomach growls out of protest. The coffee alone is not enough to satiate my hunger today so I seek sustenance in the faint glow of the refrigerator.

The smell of bacon and eggs is enough to lure even the most elusive sibling out from the depths of the far rooms. Before long the table is once again full of bodies and the clatter of forks on plates. There is no deep discussion, only comfort food and familiar company. Bacon and eggs for the soul. Sometimes it's just that simple to have a moment of grace.

We finish up the meal and wordlessly go into the routine of clearing the table, doing dishes, and picking up after ourselves. Lacey's been quiet the entire time but I'm relieved to see she's at least eaten something. No one seems overly concerned nor curious about Silver's whereabouts and I'm not playing my sister's keeper.

I'm down to two mugs, dripping as they sit on the counter, waiting to be dried. My hands are wrinkled from the dishwater. Lacey slides up to me offering a fresh towel, as mine has become more sponge than drying mechanism. Though it would be awesome for a rat tail, I resist.

"Anna," she starts quietly. "I need to talk. Privately."

I cast a glance her way and then to the others carefully, giving a nod. "Let's finish up, we can go for a walk." She nods, a small breath of relief escaping her lips.

Chores done, we grab our coats and slip down the stairs. The boys are watching television and don't seem to notice. The sun has warmed up the air a bit, and the birds are chirping. It's not altogether unpleasant.

More silence. This girl really likes to mull over her words. I debate between pushing the conversation just to get it over with or trying to avoid it all together. It's been one of those days.

"So?" I leave the air open. Another half a block passes before she quits looking at her feet.

"I saw the paper." That's all she says.

Another half block passes. I wait.

"Mom wasn't the first." It's a statement. A confession.

"The first what?" I want to be entirely clear of the direction this conversation is taking.

"The first person I made sick." She returns to staring at her thrift store shoes as we plod along.

"Explain." It's the best response I can give without passing premature judgment.

"Well... it's like this." Plod. Plod. Plod. "I spent a while working at a nursing home. Full care type stuff, hospice wing and all."

I nod.

"And these people were so... pathetic. So... lonely. No one would come to see them unless something dreadful or dire happened. So, I arranged visits."

"What do you mean?" Eyebrow arched in full inquisitor mode.

"I... *ARRANGED*... reasons for people to come and visit them," she finishes up with a sigh. "It was easier then. No one really cared. No one was looking. They were on lists of medications as long as my arm. Tweak one, miss a day or two of another, and it would be enough to send them just a little off kilter... in a fixable way, of course."

It was kind of brilliant in a faux-angel-of-death kind of way.

"It filled a need," she went on. "They got to see their loved ones. They got to have some peace. For a little while, they weren't alone. I tried only to do it when things were already hopeless. That way if there was a mistake... well... no suspicion."

I still didn't have much to say other then nodding, listening, as we walked. The ear seemed to be what she was looking for most, not an opinion.

"The thing is... people started to talk. And that's when it got sticky."

"The administrators were on to you?"

"No no, it wasn't the staff. It was the patients. They started talking, the ones that got better. Telling their friends about their odd mishaps and how their families finally came. Let's just say the elderly may not always seem the sharpest on their decline, but it didn't take long for a couple of them to do the math. When they got sick, what shift it was, how easy it was for them to pull out of it once they were back on their regular program. They noticed the patterns to the 'mishaps'..."

"And?" I wasn't quite following.

"And they started contracting me," she said, simply.

"Wait, what? What do you mean *contracting*?"

"They asked me to *arrange* visits for them. So their family would come and see them again." A heavy sigh escapes her lips. "It got out of hand."

"How so?" My mind stumbles over the revelation coming out of my innocent little sister's mouth. Another one. We Shaw women were not to be trifled with. My fight for justice, Silver's fight for power, and Lacey's fight for mercy. A macabre little tribe are we.

"They all wanted *in*. And that was the trouble. Not all of them were truly sick, or truly in need. But if I refused, they were ready to blackmail me. It was too much. I couldn't in good conscience hurt people the way I needed to in order to fulfill their petty wishes. They were willing. More than willing to suffer to see their grandchild one more time, but it... it was just..." She trails off, her voice cracking softly.

"Wrong?" I offer. She nods with a big sniffle.

"I had to leave there. I didn't want to go back to that type of facility either. I knew someone would find out. They would be able to *tell*. To smell it on me. To smell my disease." She shudders and it's not from the cold. "I swore I would stop that stuff. That I wouldn't do it again. It was too risky. And then mom..." Her words stop.

"Mom, what?"

"All she did was sigh, Anna. Sigh and look out the window, longingly. Like she was waiting for something. Waiting for someone. Someone to finally come home, walk through that door and be happy to see her. Maybe she was looking for forgiveness, maybe she just wanted the comfort of something familiar, I don't know. But she missed you. She missed all of you."

Plod. Plod. Plod. Now I'm the one watching my feet.

"It wasn't the way..." is all I can manage. But I know what she did, despite being wrong, was the only way that we would all come back again. Bitter-sweet homecoming at its finest. We were coming up on the block mark, nearing the duplex yet again. "Once more?"

She nods. I'm glad. The walking helps me process the day's events. I glance up at her shabby chic lot and see the curtains move from the front windows. The silhouette looks James-shaped. I watch the window as long as I can. The curtain doesn't stir again.

"Lacey, tell me about this boy trouble." Changing the topic seems like a good idea and the puzzle of Lacey's suitors has been bothering me for some time. The puzzle has not yet come together for me.

She spits out a laugh and shrugs. The tone is sharp, nasal. "What is it you want to know that you don't already?"

"I don't know, I just feel like I'm missing something. Tell me again... please?" Merrily we plod along.

Heavy sigh number two escapes her lips.

"They all leave. No, wait. That's not accurate. They don't stick around long enough for it to even be considered leaving." Her shoulders drop as we walk along. She's turning inside herself, trying to hide from reality.

"Yes, but what happens?"

"Well, typically it's like this... Meet super dreamy boy with sparkly eyes and dashing smile. Become smitten. Muster up courage to go out on a date. Never hear from him again. That's really all there is to tell, I'm afraid."

"That's it?"

"That's it." She sounds distant, detached. I glance back at the house from down the street and see the curtains shift yet again.

"What was it like for you and James growing up?" The hazy pieces of a long lingering suspicion start to take shape.

"I don't know. Typical, I guess. He ran interference for me with dad most of the time. Big brother keeping me safe and warm."

"Warm?" I see small danger robots dancing through my head.

"He liked to come curl up with me at night," she shrugs. "I didn't mind really... Until we got older. It was comforting usually. At least that way I had someone there if..."

"If?"

"...If dad came around." *Damn it.*

"Oh Lacey, I'm so sorry. I thought he knocked that shit off by the time you came in to the picture." Another scar that would never truly heal.

"It only happened a few times. I know you had it

117

worse." Her tone says comfort but that is the furthest thing from my mind.

"We all made do, we had to. Ancient history." *Reroute the conversation, just do it.* "What did James think of your boyfriends?"

Lacey stops cold in her tracks to stare at me. A look I can't begin to describe crosses over her face as the color falls from her cheeks.

"Why? Why would you ask that?"

I just look at her. Waiting. Knowing.

"He... he didn't like them. He always told me they weren't good enough for me. That I deserved the best. Someone special." Her frown lines catch in the shadow of the early afternoon sun. "He said he'd kill them if they ever hurt me. But they hurt me. Again and again and again. I fall for it every time, thinking maybe this time it will be different. And it isn't. And I hurt. And where the hell is big brother?"

I know where big brother has been. I know *exactly* where big brother has been.

-24-

The way I see it, there are two choices. Stand and see things out, or get the hell out of dodge and live to forget the tale. The stars are aligning in a manner most unfitting to our situation. Visions of the modern day O.K. Corral dance through my head. Fire, tear gas, helicopters with spot lights, violent dogs braying in the dark. I want no part of this. If I leave, if I just slip away, will it be leaving them to burn? The young ones who don't understand? Or if I stay will it draw more fire under the watchful eye of the overlords?

There is option number three. Silver. Silver could be the scape goat, the unwilling savior of us all. Her brashness has laid precedent. She is too confident, too cocky. Her pride will bring her down, it will be her ultimate undoing.

I'm the head of the family now... the revelation floors me. I'm the closest thing left to a leader of this broken tribe. I don't like the feel of this. I got out once but I can get out again? Sell the babies up the river for some pieces of silver? No. Make sure they're taken care of in a good manner? Maybe. They may be monsters but they're my monsters.

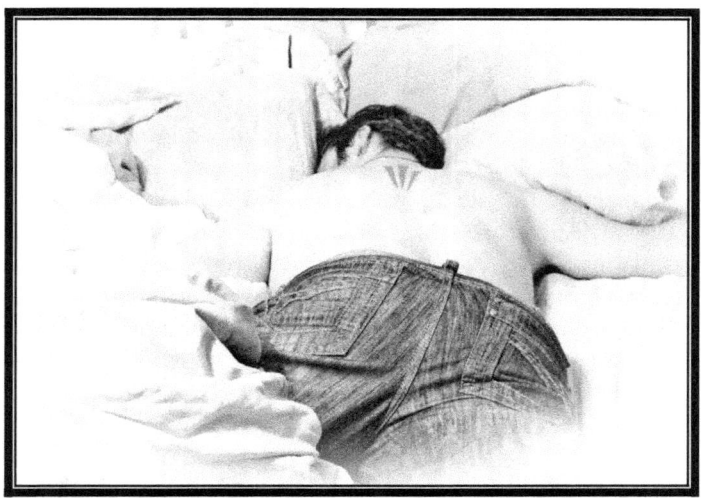

The day drones on, trying to pass the time without getting myself or anyone else in to additional trouble. Evening nears yet again and I'm stuck in this moral dilemma. The fact that I'm even considering staying around for another day is enough to make me want to run. Lacey seems less agitated after the walk and talk but James should be exhausted from pretending not to look at me. Bobby just is. Out of all of us, he is the embodiment of Zen. I can't help but wonder what his dirty little secret is in this family of monsters.

Silver being out with the ten gallon hat is another concerning factor. My sister is smart and wily and road tested but I'm hoping her prey is also of the same qualities. Hate to see a good pair of Levi's go to waste, it would be a damn shame.

Should Stephen be informed about the recent chain of events or is it best to leave him clean, unsullied, unable to testify? Too many thoughts rush my brain. The neurons cry for a drink to numb them and make it all go away. Unfortunately, now is not the time to be numb.

Think her name and she appears. Silver. I hear the jungle of her jewels from a block away. It's easy to step back in to the shadows, to observe the radiant sun known as my sister. Her gravitational pull is unrelenting as that of snake charmers and confidence men. It's hard to deny. With every step there is a chime or a bell, or a clink of the metallic. It makes a rhythmic little beat with each passing step and swirl. She knows how to make this song, she's practiced for a long time, weaving and bobbing and swaying her hips. It's a siren song.

The chimes slow as she nears the doorstep. She almost senses me, I'm sure of it. I don't try to conceal the fact that I'm there. Finally a dead stop. She studies me as I study her. I still have the advantage of the shadows to cloud her vision of my eyes.

"Sister." I hear. A nod of acknowledgment is all I allow, neither of us opting to move further. Finally her feet shift, and the spell is broken. "Waiting up for me? Wanting to hear the dish about my tall drink of water, perhaps?" The sisterly taunting isn't concealed, even for a moment.

"Maybe I am. Maybe I'm interested in the woman my little sister has become." Flick goes the tail.

"Ah, the stories of the traveling show have finally seduced you, I see. Piqued your curiosity, have they? Well I can't say as I blame you, it is a very... colorful... life wrought with mystery and intrigue."

"Well then, *darling,* we should catch up, shouldn't we?" I wonder if my teeth glint in the moonlight. The shadow of her frown betrays her as she heads for the door.

"He's fine, you shouldn't worry..." I hear floating in the air as she turns.

"Who? What do you mean?" Feign ignorance.

"The Marlboro Man, of course. He'll sleep it off, it just might take a while."

My hands reach out and snatch her before my brain has a chance to plan.

"What do you mean?" I ask her, a bit more enthusiastically. She laughs. Just looks and laughs.

"Well that got much more of a reaction than even I was hoping. You aren't crushing on the handsome steed are you?" I remain silent, jaw clenched. "Oh, you ARE! I was only bluffing!" She wiggles around in my hands, doing a bounce of self-congratulating. It stops abruptly when she realizes I'm not letting go. "Get off!" She snarls, trying to free herself once more, unsuccessfully.

I smile. And I wait until she stops struggling. It takes a moment for her to remember this game, but she calms down.

"Let's try this again." My voice is steady, even. "Silver. What did you do?"

"Nothing. Hardly anything. Not much at least..." She shifts uneasily in my hands. My grip solidifies the more she struggles; it only gives me resolve.

"Again." I look at her expectantly. The heavy sigh is the sign of compliance.

"I may have dosed him. Only slightly. He'll have a headache when he wakes up but he'll be fine." She offers this like it's an acceptable explanation.

"And *why* would you do that? I'm lost. Clarify it for me, if you would."

"Well, I have to support my habits somehow..." She lets off a small grin and weasels a roll of cash out of her pocket, despite my grasp.

"Money? That's what this is about?" The scoffing in my voice can't be concealed.

"Money... and jewelry." She pulls a large silver star out of the center of the roll but it's not one of hers. "Your crush is a Marshall. Did you know that, Anna? He was good though, he was. I hadn't caught wind of it 'til today. A pity, really..." She glances longingly at the metal shimmering in the street lights. "But it's an inconvenience, actually. What with Lacey and mom. Wouldn't want him to think there was something *funny* going on now, would we? I thought it best to remove his inspiration for coming around. Best thing for the family, of course." She smiles but all I can see is fangs.

It's all about the family.

My grip relaxes as the adrenaline runs cool in my veins. I don't let go. That would be unwise. Snakes can only strike if they have room to coil. The glitter of emerald satin and gold in the soft light is too reminiscent of scales.

"I don't think you're trying to spare the family. I don't think that's it at all."

"Oh really? Now why would you say that? After all, I'm not the one with my face plastered on the front of the local rag."

This breaks my concentration long enough for her to wrench an arm free. Her freedom doesn't last. I back her up to the wall for a little added peace of mind.

"C'mon, Anna... Clark? Did you think we couldn't put two and two together?" I lean in to her a little more, making her squeak.

"What do you mean?" The breath through my teeth escapes as a low growl.

"What's wrong, Anna? Old crushes die hard?"

I lean in again. "What the hell do you think you're talking about?"

"Oh don't tell me you don't remember. I know better than that. I know you. I'm sure it's burned into your memory, replaying on the back of your eyelids as soon as darkness falls." In this light the devil is dancing in her eyes.

"What do you know about that?" My lips almost brush her earlobe.

"Cupid never tells..."

She falls hard as I fling her away from me, like a hot rock or a nest of hornets. Looking up from all fours she laughs. Just laughs at me. It sends a chill straight through me.

"You..." I can't help but stagger backwards. "You... set me up. It was *you*?"

She laughs some more.

"Good Lord, Silver, we were only fifteen, what the he-"

A door slams. I jump and Silver is to her feet like a lightning bolt. All I can see now is Bobby's frowning face.

"What the hell is going on out here?" It's a harsh whisper, he's concerned about escalating the scene. "We keep hearing voices upstairs. We thought a couple of drunks were down here!" His eyes dart between us, trying to fill in the space between. An unsettled look is his only reward.

"Just a couple of sisters having a bonding moment and catching up on old times." Silver purrs, licking the corner of her mouth. "So nice catching up, Anna but I think it's time to retire." She makes use of Bobby as a human shield and slips into the door, my eyes sear into the back of her head.

"You okay?" Bobby gives me a worried look. It's genuine.

"Yeah, I'm fine." *Don't look him in the eyes, it'll only betray your lies.* "Go ahead and go in, it's cold out. I'll just be a minute."

He hesitates just long enough for me to shoo him, but the cold is an excellent incentive not to linger any longer than necessary.

That bitch. That lying, conniving, twisted bitch.

Never once had it occurred to me. Not once in all these years. It seems so obvious now in the rear view. It always seemed strange that he would have known where I was, where I hid when I didn't want to go home. My existence was not of his world. He wouldn't know. He couldn't know. But he did. And he knew more than that. He knew of my admiring glances, cast on the sly at class changes and unintentional path crossings. How I trailed him, quietly, at forced social events. Just watching. Just wishing. Just knowing that it would never be me, I would never be the girl he sought out in a crowd. But in private, he did. He sought me out. He sought me out and he gave me no choice.

In truth, I was mesmerized by him. By his eyes on me. The way the muscles moved under his signature jersey, showing off the shoulders and biceps he doped so hard for. It was too easy leading the lamb to the slaughter. Even with the monster of molestation waiting for me at home every night I still believed, if only for a minute, that someone might want me, might value me, might desire me.

The spell held long enough, just long enough to lower my defenses, to close the distance, to convince me that I was already powerless to the chain of events unfolding upon me. Convince me that this was my idea.

Convince me that I want it, that to deny would be cruel and unjust. Never mind that she fights. Disregard when she struggles. It's part of the game, part of the ploy. Playing hard to get, naughty girl. Don't listen when she screams, it's just drama for attention, for plausible deniability when the wrong person walks by.

It doesn't matter when there's no one to hear, no one to see and no one to save you from your darkest desire. The one thing you clung to in the dark of night, trying to find a bright spot in the depths of your personal hell; that too tarnishes and fades in the light of day. Sunlight has a way of revealing the harshness of reality. Shadows hide the soft romance of uncertainty.

The reality of the situation is again overwhelming. Despite my conditioning it takes superior concentration not to be sick. The physical repulsion flows through me like a poison. Flashes play behind my retinas. *Damn her. Damn her being inside my head.*

She got her chance to slip away. She'll run before I can nab her again, unless I want to make a scene of it. Maybe I should make it a scene. For the betterment of the family, of course. Musing over leaving her on the front doorstep of the local police tickles my brain in a special place. It's very vigilante style justice. Maybe it would earn me some karma points. Then again, maybe not.

Darkness clouds my consciousness as my thoughts turn to the painted on Levi's with the star on the belt. Alan. Putting a name to the face isn't helping matters; objectifying is so much cleaner. Don't give the meat a face, it only promotes attachment. Just hoping on his behalf for safe passage won't keep him from falling into my sister's web, her siren song has already been played. I can only wish a swift recovery and a ride to vengeance. Little Silver can get thrown under the circus caravan for all I care. She's no sister of mine now; that diseased branch of the family tree is dead. Now it just needs to be pruned.

-25-

Sharp coldness catches my attention finally, with fingers red and raw from the wind in the clear night. Shelter calls to me; the elements are unforgiving and they don't play favorites. Slipping inside, the house is nearly dark, save for the glow of the luminescent idiot box. Three bodies are comfortably curled up in front of the electronic baby sitter. One body is missing. For now.

Faint music from the back bedroom can be heard trickling over the surround sound. Flickers of light and shadow play on the carpet under the door. Movement. Lots of it. A sister in a rush. Quiet steps in the hallway are easily concealed with the ambient sounds of prime time.

The door shoves open easier than I expect. It makes a dull thud against the small of her back, sending her stumbling with a surprised yelp. A quick step and I'm inside the room with the door closed neatly behind me. She's at a temporary disadvantage but not unprepared. Clever girl hasn't gotten this far by resting on her laurels.

A swing and a flash. Before I know it, she's at me, a small Kris pulled from a garter hidden under layers of skirting. A shiny token from an exotic show or a foreign lover, no doubt. Momentum is a bitch. It takes little effort

on my part to send her flying into the bed from her own follow through. I cluck through my teeth, scolding her. Being quick is one thing, being rushed is another. People are sloppy when they're rushed. People are lethal when they're quick.

The look of fury radiating off her face as she regroups is both awesome and terrifying. The wrath of Mother Nature personified. White lit eyes clad in a red rush of skin, wild hair writhing like the many snakes of Medusa, the snarl born of her profane existence wet on her lips.

"*Bitch*," she grunts with a sputter of saliva, shades of our father flicker across her brow. Maybe it's the frothing spittle that solidifies the family resemblance. An open palm on the face slows her down for a moment, snapping her head back with a sharp staccato. Each time she comes at me, she meets the same fate until her cheeks glow red and rosy. It's apparent that her past conquests haven't been much of a struggle. It's far easier to catch flies in the honey pot than spear them through the air with needles. The knife is of no consequence; despite the ancestral bravado of her Carney act and supposed skill set, she doesn't know how to use it in a functional manner. Watching movies will only get you so far, and she should have watched more.

Wrists are vulnerable areas when the right pressure is applied at the correct angle on tender tissue, and that's true in more than just the movies. A simple twist and the faux Damascus blade drops to the floor and she pulls away, coiling like a snake ready to strike. It was easy. Too easy. Those are the last words that pass through my mind without the blaring color of a concussion attached. Sharp objects make take finesse, but blunt ones are easy for the common man's skill set. Before I can react, she makes a solid connection from a nearby wood pillar candle holder. The blow is enough to send me down and dim my lights. The last thing I remember is a pointy toed boot jingling by my head and swiftly meeting my lower ribs as the world slides behind a veil of grayness. The cloud of unconsciousness courts me until I flow into its silky iron grasp.

Floating dots in my vision greet the sharp throb coming from my hairline. The scent of latex catches in my nostrils. Band-aid. Butterfly style. I'd know it anywhere. The dim bedroom is conspicuously empty and the door is suspiciously closed. I already don't like the smell of the situation.

A free spin on the merry-go-round is my reward for sitting up too quickly, and it takes a steady hand to brace myself for a moment. My ears monitor the vibrations in the air, listening for voices, music, anything to tell me if the house is still populated. No voices, no flickers of light. Not good.

The tentative tug on the door reveals that it's not locked but it is jammed somehow. I wish this was a surprise. It's easy enough to get a decent wiggle out of the hinges without much effort. A good shoulder is all it really takes to pop the chair free. Still listening. Still nothing. *Damn it.*

Warily I step through the house, ears alert for the slightest sound of voice or body movement. They twitch from the straining but still find nothing. The living room is dark, not even the glow of the television to navigate by. A small glint in the center of the room catches my eye. It's a small silver star.

A ghost town awaits me. No sign of a struggle, no sign of a mess. For a moment I wonder if Silver just told them I tripped and took everyone out for dinner. The atmosphere isn't right; the hair on my arms stand at prickly attention as I sweep the scene for any signs. Deafening quiet greets me and the search turns up nothing. The only thing out of place is Lacey's coffee cup, knocked on its side by the sink.

A flicker of shadow draws my eye down the stairs. The tall, dark profile looming in front of the window is not familiar. Instinctively I slink to the side of the hall, staying cloaked in the permeating darkness of the house. Edging carefully towards the stairs I see the flicker two, maybe three more times before it seems to pause thoughtfully at the door. Closer I edge, step by step, easing down the stairs. The closer I get the greater risk of discovery, but the steel in my pocket reassures me.

Time slows to match the pace of my breath; quiet, easy, shallow. A stray gasp may betray my position. I make it to the door in what seems like an accelerated eon. I really wish there was a second exit to this place; being in a walk up does have some disadvantages.

The shadow still lurks beyond the door, but I can see that a back is turned towards me. Ever so carefully I ease the door knob, trying to minimize the click and praying that Lacey has oiled her hinges recently. I am rewarded for my delicate touch. Steel in hand, I slip out the door and before the profile can make a peep of protest, have my knife close to his throat.

"Don't... move." My voice comes out in a hiss. I back him closer to the house, back into the shadows. No need to draw any more attention than necessary. He complies rigidly, trying not to cut himself against my blade.

"Anna?"

Motherfucker.

"Alan?" For a moment my hand eases, but only for a moment. I pull him back under control. He lets out a small gasp through his teeth. "What the *hell* are you doing here?"

His hands shoot up in submission to show he's not armed. At least not yet. I hesitate, but lower the knife as I spin him around. The look in my eye is enough to hold him transfixed for a moment.

"I'm glad to see you're okay," he starts.

"What are you doing here?"

Silence.

"Answer my question," the knife in my hand twitches involuntarily. "Please." Amusement is not dancing in my eyes, only malicious determination.

"Silver made me before I realized it. She drugged me."

"I know."

He frowns. "I'm afraid she's already on the move. Took a while to get my head clear." He takes another look up at the dark house. "What happened?"

"I'm not entirely sure to be honest. She blindsided me with a chunk of home decor. I've been clearing my head a bit myself. When I came to I was patched up, blocked in the room and everyone was gone." At this point trust isn't really an issue. What he doesn't know he's going to find out one way or another. It's easier to pretend to play nice to further my own agenda. "Have you seen anything? Anyone leaving?"

"No, I must have gotten here after everyone already bailed. What do you think? Were they forced or did they run?"

"I don't know. I'm hoping they ran, for their sake. Silver is not to be trusted under any circumstances." My gaze locks on him and he shifts uncomfortably. His screw up may have just set off a series of events that could easily end in misfortune.

"So wait, she *told* you she drugged me?" His cognitive faculties were returning.

"Yeah, she did." I maintain my stolid unamused face.

"May I inquire as to how or why she would do that? How did that possibly come to light?"

"She was bragging," I answer carefully. The spotlight is on me now and I don't like it. "She thinks she's untouchable."

His head shakes while his fingertips massage his temples. The drugs haven't quite cleared his system, leaving his reasoning skills still visibly compromised. This makes me uneasy. Even if he does come face to face with Silver, I can't trust that his reaction time is adequate or his response even appropriate.

"Look, you still look kind of rough. No offense, but maybe you should go back to your fortress of solitude and file some paperwork or something. I can handle her."

"I can see that," his eyes pointedly focus on my fresh butterfly. My face flushes hot but it's concealed in the night.

"Cheap shot. Happens now and then, right?" He flushes this time, I'm watching for it. "She's had two lucky shots today. I'm planning on ensuring she doesn't have any more. Her luck has run out." My thumb slides absentmindedly along the spine of my blade, caressing it like a worry stone. I don't even realize I'm doing it until I catch his eyes following the movement. Careful Anna, careful. The knife clicks shut and slides back in my pocket. *Move along, cowboy, nothing to see here.*

The look trailing up my arm back to my eyes says enough. He may not know the details but he suspects. Just because Silver got the drop on him once doesn't mean he's an idiot; after all she got the drop on me too. This I must not forget.

"What I don't understand," he shifts, trying to

change the subject. "Is why she'd bother to just drug me."

"Time." It's really quite simple.

"Why?" A frown spoils his pretty face. I seem to make that happen a lot.

Words are not necessary; a few simple pantomimes that indicate him plus me, standing in front of the house talking, means no one is looking after my dear sister.

"*Sonofabitch*." His head literally hangs in shame. It's a rough day for the Marshall.

"The longer we stand here and talk, the longer it's going to take you to get your star back. I should be going anyhow."

"Oh hell no."

"Hell no, what? Don't waste your chivalry on me." The predictability of his response, while almost cute, is going to turn tiresome in a hurry if he insists that I either stay put or that he comes with me, or any combination thereof.

"I'm not letting you just walk away. You're my best chance at bringing her in."

Predictable enough.

"I don't think it's really up to you. I don't think it's up to you at all. I know Silver better than you, yes. All the more reason you need to go back to your office, push some papers and call for backup if you absolutely feel it's worth the taxpayer's money." I actually manage to make his jaw twitch.

"I don't think you understand me. You're not going alone, if at all. And if you resist, I'm taking you in as an accessory."

"The *hell* you are." I'm one threat away from a growl. "I'm not dicking around anymore with this, I'm out of here." Too bad my keys aren't in my pocket. Must have come out in the scuffle. Shit.

My car is gone too. Double shit.

The surprise flashes in my eyes. By the time I look

back up, I can see he knows I'm defeated. It's his way or nothing. This does not please me in the least.

"My truck's around the corner," is all he says.

Bounding down the road in no particular direction. Metaphor for life. My life at least. He is bound and determined to get somewhere, anywhere, quick. The interior of his cab proves a distracting study between alternating theories on Silver's whereabouts. Plain work truck, medium duty, no particular bells and whistles other than power windows. It's lackluster to say the least.

The scanner mounted carefully under the dash does expose a police association, or at least that of a local volunteer firefighter. Disappointing that a man of such a high caliber travels in such an average steed. So much for movie depictions of all the hottest technology being at the fingertips of law enforcement. Something still seems to be missing.

"Do you have a gun?" Hell of an icebreaker.

"Yes." His eyes focus even harder on the road.

"Where? This doesn't look much like a first response type vehicle."

"Don't worry about it." I can see his jaw clench. "And this is my personal truck, I'll have you know. I couldn't exactly use the company car."

"Oh that's right! You're *undercover.*" I resist the urge to laugh... mostly. A small chuckle does manage to escape my lips. He doesn't seem to take offense; in fact I see a faint curl to the corner of his mouth.

"It's on a need to know basis. Just don't worry, I'm covered." I'm starting to suspect that the day's turn of events has undermined his confidence. This is not a good thing.

"I need to know I can count on you."

"Count on me?"

"This... You... The swagger is all gone. You look

like you've been rode hard and put away wet. If you're going to try and get the drop on Silver, you have to be sharper. If she's in your head, I can't trust that you'll react properly."

"She's not in my head."

"She's an enchantress. Of course she's in your head." I feel my mouth pucker just saying those words.

A laugh and a snort resounds from the other side of the truck.

"Is that what you think? That she's be-spelled me?" He doesn't stop laughing. My mouth puckers more.

"She seems to have that gift with the male gender. Don't be ashamed, she's quite capable of being exotic when she wants to be."

"Don't worry about my attraction to her. It doesn't exist, it's fictional. That's probably why she caught on to me anyhow. It's hard to pretend to be enraptured when faced with Octopussy."

I laugh. I hate myself a little, but I laugh. The moment passes quickly.

"We're here." The truck rolls to a stop. I see my car, and the graveyard.

"How did you?..."

"We can worry about that later. I suppose it's no use to ask you to stay here and be ready to radio for backup?"

"Totally useless."

"I thought so. Come on."

-27-

It's almost exactly as I remember it. Then again, I don't suppose graveyards change much over the years. They may crumble more into runes due to lack of repair and vandalism from the local punks, but very rarely is there ever a call for a major renovation of such a site. There is a new field of stones I don't remember, but they're merely markers placed flat in the ground. No longer are the archaic statues of angels and cherubs allowed to grace the permanent resting places of the wealthy or well to do. It's all about maintenance and easy grounds keeping. Heaven forbid the fat man on the riding mower be forced to dismount and occasionally wield a weed eater in respect for the dead. Instead they get to enjoy eternal rest under the wheels of a zero turn.

I always pictured this place with Spanish moss hanging eerily on the trees, even though it doesn't exist in climates this cold. A pity really, some nice moss could really accent a graveyard. Weeping willows, almost bare from the autumnal shedding, still waver in the distance, following the little creek that cuts the cemetery into two man sections. The old graves are in the far back. The graves of the once prestigious but now forgotten where tombstones show degradation from the effects of misspent youth and acid rain.

Murky darkness has permeated the night, even the moon doesn't want to come out and shine. The moon wants no part of this. It knows better. I scan the scenery for shapes that are out of place. The years have not been kind. Lumps of tombstones are missing here or there, carving out things that look like figures and shapes in the dark. Just tricks of the eye. They're all tricks of the eye, more illusions of overactive imaginations. Some auras never change - that used to be one reason I liked this place.

That she came here isn't a surprise. That he knew to look here concerns me slightly. As children, this was often a safe place where we could go for some time alone, away from the home and away from the other cruel bastards that adults called a peer group. Trailing down the stream, following the willows, there was a small Italianate crypt with a gazebo not far from it. This is where I spent many a day hiding from the living world around me, sketch book or journal in hand. It never really mattered what time of year, the place afforded me adequate shelter and protection from the elements when needed. Very rarely was there any interruption since it was off the beaten path. It was a place only Silver and I really frequented. The boys preferred to be off on more exciting misadventures.

The old side is where I preferred to spend my time, making tracing and charcoal rubs from old stones, trying to recreate the picture of what they once looked like, how their lives passed and how they were immortalized by their loved ones. The occasional stone of a child lost to some ailment that could now be treated with over the counter drugs always gave me pause. And yet somehow, sometimes, I wish I had such an easy out.

The smell of freshly cut grass, mulched leaves and plant decay catches my nostrils. In an instant I am transported back. It was summer the last time I was here, a lifetime ago, but the smells were much the same. The night was hot and balmy so the scents were amplified in the evening air. It was later then, the darkness came later. The darkness was a gift and a curse. It was easy to be invisible in the darkness, but not being home before it set in was often a risk of personal safety if you got caught coming in the door.

That night, of all nights, I was feeling particularly resistant to authority. I wasn't going to go home until I was good and ready, even knowing what waited for me on the other side of the door. I was ready to take abuse, just to have a little more time to myself. Either way the result would be the same, so the crime should at least be worth of the punishment. To me at least.

It was late. I was alone. I was indifferent to the world around me. Of course, I was not sober, I never was at that age if I had the option. It dulled the pain in more ways than one. The poison of the night was peppermint schnapps; not a favorite but easily accessible. The medicinal tingle is something you don't easily forget.

The smell of peppermint and mulch hung heavy in the thick summer air, more dew droplets clinging to every blade of grass and leaf the longer the sun had been down. My senses were blissfully dull. Another reason I had not yet attempted the trek home. I preferred to make the walk in a moderately straight line as opposed to a looping path of stumbles. The key was to get home while still numb enough to not care but not so numb you couldn't duck and cover when necessary.

I heard the rustle in the weeds and fallen twigs, but I paid no heed. It wasn't unusual to have a neighborhood stray stroll past once the sun went down, and sometimes the regulars would search me out for a scratch or a treat. It also wasn't unusual for Silver to be sent out looking for me when I wasn't home for dinner. I preferred the company of the strays.

"Anna?" The voice that had come from behind me was not my sisters. I froze. Even now I remember the feeling, the chill that ran down my spine. Instincts should be heeded but it's funny how hope and fear can often intermingle. Sometimes the fear is one of the unknown, the things you hope for but know you'll never get. Sometimes the fear is from the sinister intentions that you feel at the cellular level. When you're a teenager sometimes lack of experience makes it difficult to tell the difference. I stayed silent then, both hoping and not hoping that I would go undiscovered. I didn't.

"Anna?" The voice whispered again, afraid to break the stillness of the night. A shifting of position was my only reply, a revelation of location. The sound of footsteps honed in on my position, and before I knew it was even a realistic possibility, he was standing in front of me with a misty, moonless night at his feet.

He approached me tentatively at first. Expecting me to lash out or run away, most likely. All the things I should have done. A cautious move and he was plunked down beside me on the steps of the structure, silent. We sat that way for what felt like a long time in the stillness. I quieted my ever aching nerves with my flask, more times than I should have.

There were no words, not at first. I sat there, as still as I could, trying not to break the spell until I felt the trace of a cool finger on the back of my neck, and then the tentative press of warm lips where the fingers had been. Motionless, I remained, like a rabbit caught in a snare. Afraid to move, to change anything, my senses suddenly amplified to hear every cricket, tree frog and crackle of branches in my vicinity. Only slight sighs and shudders transmitted involuntarily from my body. If this was a dream, I didn't want it to stop.

"What's the matter?" His breath was hot on my ear. "Don't you like me? Don't you like this?" He kissed my neck again. My shudder and uncertainty was only accentuated by his hand on my thigh. "How about this? Is this better?" He traced a line up the side of my stockings. I held back as long as I could.

"What are you doing here?" His hand paused mid stroke. I cursed myself for breaking the spell.

"I was looking for you." The ear nibbler speaks.

"Why?" My eyes ache from watching him out of the side for so long.

"Because... Because I like you. And I heard you like me too." His agenda continued to work its way up my thigh. Finally I flinched.

"No. Stop." I hated hearing myself even say those words.

"Why, what's wrong?" He managed to purr, ignoring my protests. "Just relax, we don't have to tell anyone..."

"I said STOP." I spent enough of my life being forced to do things, I didn't need one more horny jackass trying to tell me what to do or think. I made a point to remove his hands from my body. A mistake of epic proportions.

"Come on, don't be such a prude." He was back on me like a fly on shit. So much for the tender approach. Why did the young Neanderthals have to be so After School Special?

I pushed him, hard. Hard enough to knock him back and into the railing. I heard the knock of head on wood. He came back at me, engorged and enraged. I screamed at him to stop. I struck him repeatedly but at that point it didn't matter. He didn't care. He was high on adrenaline, endorphins and probably whatever performance enhancing drug helped him get through his game earlier in the night.

"Clark! NO!" was the last thing I screamed before he slapped me hard enough to knock me out. It was all over but the crying.

It took a little time after that to align my resources, but I skipped town the first chance I got and never looked back. I shouldn't have looked back. I shouldn't have come here. Everything was unraveling;

what few things I had left were spinning into miraculous disarray.

"Anna? Anna!" The male voice behind me snaps me back into the moment, I spin ready to strike. "Easy, easy... shh. What's wrong, are you okay?"

Alan. Damn it. This is why we're here. Because Silver always knew my favorite place to hide, to get away, and apparently she had a big mouth. *Twice now you betray me.* This will be the last time.

"Hey, are you okay?"

I need to physically shake my head to clear the cobwebs of memories stuck in the frontal lobes.

"Yes, I'm fine. I know where to go, follow me." I leave the flashlight Alan gave me off. She would see it coming a mile away. Though I know she is already expecting us, so there is little chance of surprise.

-28-

Rustling wind through the leaves gives us favor tonight. The hiding moon, the babbling brook and the speaking trees conceal our movements as we ease through the site. This is a double edged sword, as it makes it equally difficult to observe changes in the scenery around us. Under different circumstances this might be considered a nice, romantic walk in the autumnal eve.

Alan is right on my heels. One false step and he'll be knocking me to the ground if he's not careful. I appreciate the theory of having back up but not the lack of shadowing technique. A couple abrupt stops are enough to give him the clue to follow at a more appropriate distance. I'm unsure about this partnership. I don't feel ill at ease around him but the bottom line is that he is the Law. And the Law is not my friend, nor has it ever been. The blind eye of the virtuous never helped out the hurt and the angry kids from the wrong side of the tracks. Now I am helping one of them to capture one of us. It doesn't seem right.

The peeling paint on the gazebo is obvious even in the failed evening light. This area has not been maintained for quite some time. Moss grows on the roof, where sticks and leaves from nearby trees collect and

decay. Every memory is left to disrepair. Nearing the structure, my eyes search the darkness for a hint of a shadow against the remaining white of the railings. Surely I should be able to see her. Surely we should see something, but we don't. I stop in my tracks.

"This doesn't make any sense. I know she's here, I know she's waiting, lurking somewhere. She's watching us right now, I can feel it. Can't you feel it?"

Alan's wordless response is to scan the neighboring trees for our little fugitive in training. She already wrote the book on how to disappear; what could her final exam possibly be? Middle children could be such drama-mongers, always trying to eclipse the luster of the elder siblings and the cuteness of the younger ones.

We give the gazebo a wide berth. Best to stay on the fringes we're harder to spot that way even if it compromises our own visibility slightly. Finally I stop, just listening to the movement of nature around me. I close my eyes and let my ears reach out to the trees and the water and the grass under my feet. I hear the leaves, the occasional call of a barn owl in the distance, even passing cars on the highway far off in the night. *Focus. Closer.*

My fingers splay at my sides like antenna, feeling the shift of the wind as it plays against my body, feeling the wisps of ghosts trail through my hands on the currents of the breeze. Small chips of tree debris sprinkle my face, like sand from a dune. I can feel it in my hair, on my eyelids, brushing past my ears. My senses cast out in to the landscape around us. It's not a super-human feat, it's about knowing how to focus and feel. *Deep breath. Easy now.* Where would she...

"The crypt." My voice comes out in a hoarse whisper on the breeze, enough to make Alan jump. Somehow the revelation is also a surprise to myself.

I direct him around the back while I stalk close to the front of the structure. The petite mausoleum is intimidating in the night. It's unnatural to be here, amongst the dead, following through on a mortal human drama. There will be no peace for them tonight. Tonight they may feast on the blood of the living.

Images of pagan gods grace the small pediment, in scenes of victory and war. Hard-handed symbolism adorns every piece of stone and metal from the miniaturized Corinthian column tops to the corroded steel rivets which ornament the thick metal strapping. This place was not created to be forgotten. How disappointed the tenants must be that their fortress of immortal glory has been left to ruin, decay, and shoddy landscaping. In death we are equal, no matter how fine the burial shroud and shrine. Ashes to ashes.

The heavy, iron strapped doors are cracked, ever so slightly. Even the stiff breeze doesn't convince them to sway. They did not get this way accidentally; the ancient padlock hangs sadly in disrepair. In the far corner of the crack, a slight flicker of light. This is the place. This is the place where a chapter will end. It's been a week of endings. Maybe for once we can all be at peace, like the dead.

I run a finger along the edge of the outer door, feeling for a good gap to slide my fingers in. A slight tug reveals that the hinges are not eager to move after many years of rest. They protest my tentative nudge; there will be no sneaking. Another deep breath.

The weight of age groans in protest as both hands pull it open to shield my body, clearly announcing my presence to all around. This is one occasion that makes me wish I was the type who liked to carry a gun. A small set of wood doors meets my eyes. I'm just in the antechamber. I puzzle for a second about how big the crypt appeared from the outside; apparently its actual size is hidden in an optical illusion. Or maybe I just fell through the rabbit hole. If only it were that easy.

The second door swings easily, as it has not been

abused by the elements and generations of young blooded tomfoolery over the long years. A slight peek at the door reveals a skirt hem resting on the marble floor, in a flicker of what I can only assume is candle light.

"Come in, we've been waiting..." No amount of steel in my hand is going to make me *want* to go through that door. Knife concealed but at the ready, I push and the inner chamber door yields easily.

Lacey sits cowered in the corner, head in her hands, trying her best not to cry and failing miserably. Silver greets me with a large, toothy grin, almost reptilian in nature by the candle-light. I stand, poised for whatever she has ready to throw at me. I know she is prepared.

A knife whistles by my ear. That wasn't exactly what I had in mind. I mange not to flinch, it would have been too late anyhow. Silver is still smiling. *Bitch.*

"So. What now? Where do you want this to go? How does this family reunion resolve?"

"Well, I've thought about that a bit at this point, as you might imagine." She begins to pace back and forth in front of ages of death markers. "This is all very... dramatic. Picturesque. Deliciously morbid. It's really more than I had hoped for." Back and forth, spinning around fixed-blade in her hands. I keep an eye on her wrists, anticipating a wind up.

"That's a very flowery way to say nothing in particular. You seem to have a gift for that." Shadow flickers in her eyes.

"Don't bait me, Anna. You're in no position to be in command of this situation. I'm going to be head of this family. In my likeness they will rise. We have limitless potential if we bind together."

"What the hell are you talking about?"

"Oh come now, Anna. You know exactly what I'm talking about. We all have these *tendencies*. You and I both know it. I say it's time to rise together and capitalize upon our strengths. It's time to band the broken." Pace,

pace, pace. The mastermind is truly at work. Lacey whimpers again.

"Where are the boys?" There are no signs of them and this chamber isn't big enough to cleverly conceal additional bodies unless they're in urn form. The only way out is through me. I alone stand between Silver and her salvation.

The chill of the crypt makes my skin clammy. A fine layer of moisture clings to me the longer I stand here, accentuating the must and mold that has helped along cellular decomposition of the occupants over the years.

"The boys were being *difficult*. I had them wait in the car." Evil smile. Evil, evil smile. The game of cat and mouse is wearing on my nerves.

"What did you do to them?" *Keep your voice even, she feeds off of emotion like an energy vampire.* She'll exploit any weakness she can find.

"They're fine. For now. Don't worry, I just left them to think over my very persuasive argument for taking our show on the road. Would you believe that Bobby is going to be the hardest nut to crack? I didn't think that boy had much of a spine in him, but he can take a hit, that's for sure." She talks like she's talking about an inanimate object. Detached, no sign of humanity.

"And what about her?" My eyes stray to Lacey, still crumpled in the corner.

"Well, she was being a bit difficult as well, but we came to some terms, didn't we dear?" Silver rests her hand on Lacey's golden locks. I see the faint shudder as Lacey winces from the touch. She raises her face long enough for me to see raised red welts on the side of it, sharpening the color of her already moist eyes. Sister on sister violence seems to be the evolving theme of the evening.

"Let her go, Silver. She doesn't need this. You and I can settle this without her."

Silver doesn't relinquish her contact with Lacey. Lacey just eyes me, hurt pouring through her sockets and burning in to my soul. If I didn't know better I would swear I see her lean into Silver's touch.

"See, the thing is..." Silver's hand drops as she starts to pace again. "She doesn't trust you." My face flushes red.

"What?"

"She knows, Anna. She knows about you. The local news. What you did to Alan." She gives a pause long enough for my temper to peak. "In fact, she can't believe how you went after me the way you did. It really was rather *crazy*. Wasn't it now? We've been discussing what to do with you, actually. We don't want you to hurt people any more, dear. And we especially wouldn't want you to hurt yourself."

My brain flashes hot with rage, there's no way to conceal it.

"What the FUCK are you talking about, Silver? You're the one that drugged Alan. You're the one with a chain of bodies following you from coast to coast. YOU are the one that came at me. The only psychopath in this room is YOU."

A maternal glance is cast at Lacey. "See, I told you she would say that. Poor girl, she's delusional. Mother's death must have just made... her... snap." Lacey whimpers again. "Shh shh shh, don't worry my dear. I won't let her hurt you." Her condescending tone hangs thick in the air.

What would it take to close the distance? Not much. What would it take to ensure that Lacey did not become collateral damage? Too much.

"Let's get the boys."

"What?" Silver stops, perplexed.

"The boys, let's go get them. You want a family meeting? You got it. Lacey, go get the boys."

Confusion shows on Lacey's face, unsure if it's safe to move, uncertain of what's unfolding. *Get out Lacey, just get out.* Let me take care of the rest. Please, take the hint. Please. She stirs slightly, eyes fixed on Silver.

"This is what you want, isn't it? The band of merry murderers? Well it's not going to happen unless they come along willingly; otherwise, you risk insubordination at every turn."

Silver is frowning now, lost in thought for a moment. I wait for her to put the pieces together, to come to a similar conclusion of her own. Her head cocks; she doesn't look at Lacey.

"I suppose you're right. Go get them." She throws my car keys at Lacey, but they clatter on the floor at her feet. "Go ahead, take them. Go get your brothers."

She doesn't wait to be told again. The keys are in her hand almost immediately as she bolts out the door. No looking back. Only then do I remember Alan is still lurking outside. I hope he does the right thing.

It only takes a minute, a brief glimmer of time before I hear the slam of iron doors behind us. *Son of a bitch.*

"What the hell did you DO?" The exclamation resounds in stereo.

"Did you put her up to this?" I scream at Silver.

"Did you have this planned?" Silver screams at me.

Pause. Regroup.

"Wait," I start. "You expect me to believe this wasn't all part of your nefarious, elaborate plan?"

"First of all... do you think I talk like that? And secondly, no, of course not. Why the hell would I want to be locked in here?"

Two siblings enter, one sibling leaves? Assuming, of course, whoever is on the outside has the intentions of letting the victor out. It would be too easy to cut your losses and let it be one of the cities unsolved mysteries. I hope to hell that someone is just buying time to find help. I hope to hell that someone is on my side.

It's difficult to know what to do when your survival is on the line from multiple threats. Sure, Silver is here, with her knives and her Cheshire grin, but there's also the matter of the impenetrable fortress I am now entombed within. As it stands, even if I win, odds are I lose.

We both stand motionless but guarded, reassessing our options. Combining forces to escape seems unlikely and unnecessary. Silver needs me out of the way if she wants to successfully become the pied piper of wayward children. The very thought shakes me to my core. I'm not always proud of the life I lead, but I've done what I've had to for survival, and to give others a similar chance to thrive. It's never been out of novelty or boredom. It's not something I want to do to pass the time, count the hours and the days, or even keep tally of. If these situations didn't keep presenting themselves to me, I'd be all the happier to avoid them. But the fact is that they do. And the fact is that I'm not afraid to do what needs to be done to nip the genetic scourges from the face of civilization. Consider it a public service. My service tonight is to make sure another predator doesn't make it back on the street. My survival is no longer a concern.

A funny thing happens when you have nothing left to lose. For years I never cared if I lived or died. Dark thoughts and attempts at taking my own life happened more times than I want to remember. The cuts on my wrists weren't always just cries for help. Sometimes they were cries for salvation. Please God, carry me through to the other side, I'm tired of this fresh living hell. But I never succeeded, no matter how hard I tried to convince myself that I was determined. And now, at this moment, I know. I know there was a reason. It need not be divine or even spiritual, but it does serve a purpose for the few. As I stand here now, a sheep for the slaughter, I have one last chance at redemption. It doesn't matter where my soul lies by the end of the night - if I can give my last breath knowing that I saved the few, the tender, the broken.

Silver cannot be allowed to walk these hallowed grounds of final rest. She has no right to be among the living; she has walked too closely in the footsteps of our father. The pain she brings is for her own joy and merriment. For her own satisfaction and power. There is no noble cause. There is no rhyme or reason. It's a sickness, a perversion, a need that she has to fill. People don't change. They don't turn over a new leaf and ignore a part of their being that is so integral to identifying who they are. It's impossible. And the longer the urges are suppressed, the more intense the itch will become. The longing. The cravings. The need. Eventually we all regress back in our primal states.

I take no joy in the solemn duty laid before me. To slaughter your own sister is not noble, no matter how many lives it may save. Maybe if I can do this one thing. This one thing to right the wrongs that I have transgressed against my family, over the years. Maybe then I can finally find my own peace among the graves.

Lost in your thoughts is not a good place to be when you're trapped in an inescapable box with a tigress.

The searing pain of my skin being parted by steel catches my attention. Silver has beat me to my own conclusion. *The bitch has overstepped her bounds for the last time.* A futile swipe at the whirling dervish yields me nothing but a hand full of air. She had her chance at a cheap shot, I should have expected she wouldn't wait for a fair fight. I'm ready to level the playing field.

Silver comes in for another swipe, wagering that I'm still reeling. Silly, silly girl. I slap her hard, increasing her momentum towards the quickly approaching wall. It's a passive move, really. Much easier to use someone's own body against them when the occasion arises. Strength can be neutralized with a few simple steps. What she has in willowy reach can be used against her if she can't control her sinuous limbs. She manages to throw on the brakes before she fully presses against the cold stone wall. I can't help but be disappointed.

She may be bad at the frontal attack, but I'm sure coming up from behind would better suit her style; I'll not give her that chance. A kick aimed for my knee manages to just brush my shin. The contact gives me enough time to grab her hemline and capture her balance with a solid tug. This leaves a thrashing set of very angry feet in very close proximity to all of my tender regions. My attempts to gain better control meet nothing but resistance and it's only a moment before she manages to wiggle free of my weakened hold.

Time slows like dripping strands of honey when adrenaline is pounding through every synapse, ensuring primal survival. Even the quickest moves seem to break down in slow motion, giving time to react and counter. Unfortunately, time plays favorites to no man. It's no easier to react any quicker than my opponent but I know when to brace myself for a blow.

I manage to put a nice dent in her ribs while fielding a particularly aggressive offensive. The yelp is satisfying to my ears, like cool water on a parched tongue. I can always get therapy later to work on these issues, but for right now, I have to channel my share of the evil that we both have burning inside us. I have to feed the monster. The feel of flesh bruising beneath my fingertips is all it takes. It awakes. It breathes inside me.

Savage nature takes over my hands. My mind goes blank with white hot rage. I will likely not remember what transpires at my own hands on this night, I will only know the outcome and a blurry recollection of events. I find my hand full of hair, and Silver's head is attached to it. She screams in rage and pain, clawing at my arm and face. It only makes me pull harder.

Make her scream. Make her twitch. Make her cry out in pain and beg for mercy and salvation and all that is holy to the gods of the nations. It will do nothing but incense me. There is no mercy left in me. Not tonight.

My hands tear at her between blows from my increasingly bloodied knuckles. She fades in my grasp after the relentless onslaught; the smell of sweat and blood and captive bodies permeates my senses. It's hard to breathe in this tightly closed crypt after such exertion. The air is thick and moist, much like my shirt which clings to me despite its newly tattered state. It weighs heavy on my lungs.

Silver is down. For now. Shallow breaths escape her parted lips. In the pale light she resembles something from a fairy tale or folk lore. Skin pale from life draining out of her, lips ashen from trauma, hair nested in bloody ratted knots, green scales glistening in the light of the flame. A trickle of blood trails from the corner of her mouth, dripping into a small pool on the floor. It will stop eventually. This all will stop eventually.

This sealed room is unyielding. Even if Silver becomes aware again, there's no telling if it will matter. Starvation is an ugly way to die but maybe it's a befitting fate for two twisted freaks like us. Suffocation may be a bigger concern. The must in the air signifies a lack of substantial air movement over the years. The spinning in my head could be from a number of things right now, but if it doesn't stop soon I have another set of worries.

No one can hear me scream. I don't even try. The only thing I'm safe from right now is nuclear fallout. Barring that, I'm screwed if I'm forced to stay in this room. I say a small thanks to my tumultuous upbringing that I'm not the claustrophobic type. Yet. That could quickly change with the ever thinning air quality.

Quietly I sit; waiting, breathing, keeping an eye on Silver as the shallows breaths push in and out of her chest. I could end it. I could end it all now but I'm not sure that solution is good enough. I'm not sure she deserves such mercy. She should be held accountable for her sins.

I keep myself busy trying to remember the final scene from Romeo and Juliet, picturing it on a more sinister scale. *Two sisters, alike in dignity...* No, not really. *Two sisters, alike in blood lust...* Well, maybe.

The longer I have time to sit and reflect, the less I want to believe that this is it. That after all this, everything, I get locked inside my eternal resting place with a crazy sister and a candle threatening to go out. This is the point where many would start to make bargains with God. Not me. It's worthless. Right now I would have better luck with the Devil. At least he gets results.

Darkness tries to close in on me but I resist. Oxygen deprivation, exhaustion, blood loss; I'm not really sure which one is pulling me into its slumbering grasp. It feels like a conspiracy that I can't fight. It seduces me, soothing the hurts and the terrors in my mind. Pulling me quietly into the velvety grasp of slumber once again. Despite my will to fight it doesn't take long before the room flickers from gray to black. The last thing I vaguely feel is my head slump back and hit the moist stone wall.

-29-

"Anna. Annnna? Anna, can you get up?"

A fog looms in my consciousness. *Leave me alone,* my body screams, *can't you see that I'm tired?* I grunt in protest.

"Anna." *Nudge.* "Anna?" *Push.* "Anna?" *Shake.* My eyes unwillingly begin to part, trying to pull in to focus the hazy night.

"What the hell are you doing in my bedroom?" is my only reply. I swear I can audibly hear the sound of frowning around me.

"I don't know, she seems really out of it." I hear the voices tickling on the breeze in my dreams. My eyelids flutter in response. "Let's get her outside." The dead weight of my body repeatedly oozes towards the floor, making it difficult to lift me in one tidy package. I try to help but I don't seem able to. Everything about me feels limp and lifeless. Maybe I should stay that way. Maybe I'm close now.

The cold ground outside is enough to get my attention after being trapped in the stale, moist box. It doesn't take long for my wits to come about me. A breath of fresh air helps tremendously to clear my head and regain my bearings. Flickering lights make it difficult to focus on my surroundings without much other ambient light around. I know where I am but I'm still disoriented. Not everything is making sense yet.

A glimmer of soft gold at a nearby tree catches my eye. Even in the flickering, fading lights I can see Lacey standing there, looking distraught. I try to hold my hand up to wave but it has other ideas at the moment. A limp wristed twitch is all I can muster right now. The worried look on her face does not soften.

"Anna? Are you feeling any better now?" A voice. It's male. It's familiar. It's... Alan. *Flashing lights. Alan.* Of course. Bastard ratted me out.

"I'm fine," is all I can manage to eek out through the scowl on my face. I expect to see the flash of handcuffs as soon as I'm well enough to be on my way. Instinctively I start scanning for exits. One thing I notice is that I only see Lacey, not the other siblings. The other thing I can't help but note is that I am completely, unequivocally surrounded. Here we go again.

"Where is Silver?" The first coherent words out of my mouth and Alan frowns.

"She was in pretty bad shape when we got to her, Anna. You really worked her over good. She's at the hospital now, under guard. What the hell happened in there?"

My aching jaw clenches. It's hard to be forthcoming when you aren't sure what you're admitting to.

"I did what I had to do." Simple. It's that easy.

"What do you mean?"

I guess it's not that easy.

"What the hell do you think I mean, Alan? She tried to kill me, yet AGAIN today, so I put her down like the dog she is. *Bitch.*" I spit a faint trace of blood out for effect. Are you sure she's really under guard?" The concern infiltrates my tone more than I intend.

"Yes, she's in custody. She'll be Mirandized and everything when she finally comes to again." Still frowning. It's not a look that suits him. He looks older when he frowns. Rough. Worn. Worried.

"Don't frown at me. Why the hell did you lock me in there, you asshole? You know she's crazy." No wonder he looks so worried. He won't even look at me. He knows he was bad.

"I did what I had to do." He answers quietly.

"What the hell kind of reason is that?"

"It had to be done, I was out of options. I had to assess the situation and make sure of what was going on. The minute Lacey came running out, I knew what I had to do. I knew you would be okay..." His voice wavers slightly. "At least I hoped you would." Another frown, this one directed at himself.

Pain shoots through my arm as I go to move myself, I can't stifle the wince. Ah yes, the knife wound. Thankfully the only considerable one, and it's just a flesh wound at that. That kitten seriously needs her claws clipped. The grimace makes the injury obvious. Alan only now notices that I'm bleeding my own blood.

"Let's get you to the ambulance."

"What? This? Oh no, no need. Don't worry about it, there are more important things to contend with right now." He doesn't budge. "Such as, where are my brothers? And am I free to go?"

Another frown. *Damn it.*

"Well?"

"We don't know where your brothers are yet. And while you're not being held on any charges, due to the brutal nature of what happened to Silver, it would be best if you didn't leave town for a few more days." I ignore him.

"Did you talk to Lacey?"

"I tired. She wouldn't say much once she got out of there. Poor thing seems pretty shaken up. Any idea what happened to her?"

"Let's see. Before or after Silver dragged her in the crypt as bait to ambush her sister?" I'm not being helpful but I don't care. I need to talk to my little sister and I absolutely do not need him around to make her clam up.

Sitting on the cold earth is making me start to

ache more than I already was. The sprinkling mist from above is not helping matters. Twinkling scenery starts to festively glisten like a light show with the flashing hazards, police lights, and ever increasing precipitation. Alan continues to stonewall me on Lacey.

"ALAN. We need to go somewhere else. I would like a hot shower, to get my wounds dressed, and most importantly, to talk to my sister. I'm concerned about the safety of my siblings. Other than Silver, of course. *May she rot in hell."* I try not to spit.

"I've still got my truck. I'll go get Lacey. It'll be a cozy ride but it should be fine."

"Scratch the truck for the moment. I'm going to the gazebo, bring her over there. And I need to talk to her *alone.* OK?" He nods but looks displeased. I guess that's just too damn bad.

Lacey approaches slowly, still hesitant after the events that have transpired. Her body language is totally shut down. Hopefully getting the information I need from her won't be a fight. We look at each other for a few hard seconds. She tries not to look at the rips and stains on my shirt.

"I saw what you did to her. Why would you do that?..." It comes out in a whisper.

"I did what I had do. She gave me no choice. You know that, right?" Her half nod is not encouraging. "What I need to know from you is where Bobby and James are. What did Silver do to them?"

Lacey's eyes well up in a pool of tears on the cusp of spilling over. "I begged her not to... it wasn't right..." Is all she can muster before the dam bursts and she throws her face into her hands to hide the sobs.

"Lacey. Listen to me. Are they still alive? Are they okay?" She manages a small nod. A wave of relief washes over me. "Where are they? Can you show me where they are?"

She hands me the keys to my car.

It takes a little effort to retrace our steps and find my car in all of the confusion. The local officers don't make it any easier to navigate. Cars and men seem to block my path at every turn. I'd rather not have their help. Finally, I spot my car off to the side of one of the lanes. No one has even bothered to look at it or notices that it's there. I'm not sure if this is a good or bad omen.

I take the light Alan gave me and shine in the back of the car. Nothing, not even a trace of them. Where the hell did she leave them? Confusion crosses my face and I shine the light on Lacey. Wordlessly she points to the trunk. *Fan-fucking-tastic.*

The key, as usual, gives me grief just long enough to send me in to a panic. A final shove and twist and the bitch of a lock finally gives, revealing something I never wanted to see in this life: two of my brothers in the trunk of my car; bloodied, gagged and half frozen to death. Just add that to the long list of issues to give to a therapist someday.

Bobby and James blink up at me, eyes adjusting to the ray of light beaming into their retinas. They are crammed in my trunk like a pair of sardines. I know my trunk is roomy but this is pushing the limits. At least they're not big guys; it worked out better for their sake for once. Silver managed to restrain their hands and feet haphazardly, but there was no real way to wiggle free in the tight space. Duct tape shines over their mouths. *Cold hearted bitch.* I ease the tape off of the two before starting on the bonds; a gasp for air is the first thing either of them do. Thank god neither of them has something as simple as an allergy or I would be peeling tape off an asphyxiated brother.

The cops appear to have confiscated my knife in the process of removing me from the crypt. Good know now, pigs, thanks a lot. I have nothing to cut with so undoing the bonds takes a painfully long time given the situation. Finally, I manage to get Bobby loosened up enough so that I can pry him out of the trunk. This gives James more room to maneuver; getting him out is a piece of cake.

They stand there trembling, leaning on my rear bumper in the faint glow of the flashlight, huddled together for warmth. They don't look ready to talk and I don't have much in my car in the way of emergency supplies. I'm ill prepared for these cold weather regions but I'm hesitant to send them to the ambulance and stir up a whole new pot of questions. As it stands, Alan seems to have forgotten about me for the moment. He's busy talking to a uniform in the glow of the blinking lights.

Screw it. It's time to get out of here. I tell them all to get in the car, but when I turn around Lacey is gone.

-30-

The things we do not see. Revelations that happen under the cloak of darkness, the in between times, the moments our heads are turned. The feeling that something important you should know has passed you by yet somehow missed the universal cue. A whisper out of earshot, a knowing glance behind your back. It's too easy to be at the wrong place at the wrong time. What things had I not seen? What whispers had I not heard? What pointed glances were exchanged by co-conspirators?

My only choice is to grab Bobby and James and get the fuck out of here. We can figure out the rest once we're on the road. The last thing they want to do is get back in my car, but it's just too damn bad. At least I let them upgrade their seating choices. Bobby claims shotgun and James curls up in the back, looking more disgruntled than usual. If Lacey was instrumental in his earlier ride, his whole world view could easily be crumbling. His *precious* has possibly turned on him.

Oddly, it doesn't take much to get the car out of the cemetery unnoticed and slip away from the police activity. Their typical attention to detail never ceases to amaze me, but it has worked to my advantage on more than one occasion. No one seems to be looking for two men and a woman on a leisurely evening drive.

I follow the reflective 'H' signs on the main path through town. The nice thing about a small town is that there's only one place to go. I intend to make sure that Silver is indeed competently secured before I can be at peace for the night. Little sister I can deal with later.

Dim street lights fade as the blocks pass. My eyes stay glued to the rear view, watching for any hint of an authority figure and also providing me with the occasional opportunity to glance at James scowling into the mirror.

"Bobby, how are you doing?" Silence. "You need to talk to me. Tell me what happened." More silence. I'm tired of being gentle, I'm not a coddler. These kids are seriously starting to piss me off. Maybe they're under Silver's spell. This could be very bad for me.

A quick glance at the clear streets and I decide I've had enough. I brake hard, pulling the car to the side of the road. I can see that I have the boys attention by the whites of their eyes beaming at me in the pale light.

"I said tell me *what the fuck* happened. I'm not playing any more games. What did that hateful bitch have to say when you found me knocked out in her room?"

Silent glances. *Oh Christ, not again.* I grit my teeth. "TELL ME." James gives me the same defiant, pouting glare. Bobby's resolve finally starts to soften.

"She told us how you went after her. Unprovoked. How you man handled her outside of the house, and chased her down once she got inside. She even told us what you did to her man friend, all because you were jealous of her." His voice wavers between accusatory and unconvinced.

I laugh.

"And you believe this all, without question, from our sister the actress?"

"Well, there was the matter of the newspaper we never got resolved..."

Of course there was.

"So without a second thought, you just write me

off and sell me up the river?"

"Actually, I was the one that patched you up." Bobby still looks like he swallowed a bug.

My hand traces the aching cut on my hairline. I had forgotten about it in all the excitement. Silver had done me the favor of freshening the wound up a little bit in the scuffle. It's so much better when you don't acknowledge a wound. The minute you see it, it starts to hurt. Amazing how the brain lets you plow through things and feel invincible until the rush fades and the nerve endings start tingling again. The past few hours have not been good to me and I'm beginning to feel it in my ribs and face. I'll probably have a nice shiner in the morning and a cracked rib or two aching for good measure.

I catch a worried glance from the boys. Maybe they aren't so dedicated to mama Silver after all. Back to the inquisition.

"So there seems to be a bit of information still missing here. Silver says I attack her, you patch me up, and somehow I end up locked up in a bedroom and YOU end up locked in a trunk. Can you fill in the blanks for me a little bit, please?"

James and Bobby both shift uncomfortably.

"She said she'd kill us." James whispers from the back. "She'd kill us if we didn't go along with her. We didn't want to go and we tried to keep her from leaving the apartment. She had Lacey convinced that it was all your fault, all your doing." He takes a thoughtful pause. "It really didn't take much."

"So explain to me again how you ended up in the trunk?" *Cat and mouse. Cat and mouse.* I grow weary of prying information out of every single person I'm forced to deal with in this poor excuse of a life.

"She held a knife to my throat. That, I was willing to face. Then she whispered in my ear that Lacey was next if I didn't go along with her..." James looks like he has a bitter taste in his mouth. "Lacey went along with Silver though, she hardly protested. She even slammed the trunk..." He looks shaken.

I look to Bobby. He nods. The look in his eyes tells me it's true.

"Same thing basically to me. I didn't make her hold me at knife point thought, it wasn't worth fighting. She clearly had control of the situation."

"Did she say anything else? Any clues as to what she was up to? Any *grand* ideas of hers?" They both look confused. Apparently sis left out that part of her evil plan.

I pull the car back on the road nice and easy. It's not much further to the hospital and the boys finally seem to be behaving themselves. There is no surprise when we arrive and they refuse to go in. It's easier that way anyhow, I just need to be in and out. A bigger entourage just means more limbs to keep track of.

Again with the stink of sterile sickness. Too many trips to the hospital in too short of time. One wing I'm not familiar with is where they keep 'persons of interest' that find themselves in need of saving before they can be punished to the fullest extent of the law. Oddly enough they don't seem to have that zone well marked and I'd rather avoid alerting the staff to my presence any more than necessary. Of course, pacing the halls, one after another, isn't exactly the most subtle tactic either. What I need is a little bit of a distraction, I figure my odds are better if I check at the emergency room admission. It's likely she came through that entrance anyhow and it's even more likely that the people there won't really take note of who came looking, as opposed to a bored floor nurse who has nothing better to do than stare at the few people that wander through after hours.

Lady luck is on my side. I find a frazzled nurse on the cusp of a shift change. She remembers the call being brought in and gives me the room number as soon as I tell her I'm family. I try not to get more specific. I figure a casual stroll down the hall will tell me what I need to know; that she's there and that even if she does rally, she won't be a threat.

Of course, it's not that easy. It's never that easy. I turn the corner to catch a flicker of gold. How the hell Lacey beat me to the hospital without wheels, I have no idea. I guess I shouldn't have taken time out for the heart to heart. *Hang back. Watch and wait.* I watch her walk slowly down the hall, checking off the numbers of the rooms with her finger as she walks by. Finally, she pauses and peers in a door carefully. Her hand goes to her mouth and she looks around to see if anyone is watching. *No no dear, the coast is clear. Go ahead. Go inside.* Another cautious look and she steps out of sight into the room.

Problem number one, there appears to be no security detail. Problem number two, little Lacey is right where she shouldn't be. Problem three appears as I make my way down the hall. Silver looks entirely too well rested for my tastes. This is not going to be the resolution I had hoped for. And here comes problem number four just in time, minus the trademark cowboy hat.

I find a vantage point to observe. Alan rounds the corner to Silver's room and stops dead in his tracks. Apparently he wasn't prepared for company either. Finally, he steps into the room. If I didn't know better I'd say I saw a flicker of a smile on his face. *Wait a damn minute.*

Now I have to find a way to breeze by the room again. I can't manage to see in to it without making myself look extremely suspicious and the whole impersonating the staff thing is just too much effort. At best, I can ease up and try to eaves drop.

One would think that a hospital would be a quiet enough place to overhear a casual conversation drifting from a room, but between overhead pages and general noise echoing down the halls, I have a hard time making out what exactly is transpiring between them.

"... well I'm glad to see you're not too much worse for the wear. I'm really sorry it had to turn out this way..."

"...just glad you're safe, that's all..."

The sounds I hear are that of apology not interrogation. Rationalizing the situation is making my head spin. Alan has been playing me all along. He knew where to go because Silver instructed him to bring me there. How the hell did she work her mojo on him so quickly?

It's time to go and get out of here. I have to get out of this hospital and this town; it's full of nothing but poison. Let them finish each other off - I wash my hands of this band of lunatics.

My thoughts stray to my brothers, left patiently waiting in the car. I know James is no fan of mine. The possibility that they're all in on the same scam chills me. Maybe Silver really did have her recruitment seminar. I have to unload the dead weight and lay rubber.

Getting out of the hospital is easy. No one really noticed me on the way in and they're even less likely to care on the way out. My car is, thankfully, still where I left it. The boys however are not. *Wonderful.* I'm done playing tender of lost souls. If they're not here, they get to walk and I'm off easy. Logic dictates that I wouldn't' want them in my car anyhow. The last thing I need is carjacked by a psycho sister-lover.

I slide in to Bessie, my metal stronghold, and start up the engine. She purrs like a hyena. *Atta girl.* I'm ready to lay waste to the parking lot until the yells of "Anna, wait!!" echo behind me. *Shit.* Why is trouble always in my rear view mirror? Bobby flags me down from the parking lot. *Sigh.* I wait.

He sees my hesitation and runs for the car, frantically leaping in to the passenger's seat.

"Anna, drive! You have to drive!"

The way this day is going I'll act first and ask questions later. He slams the door and I lay on the gas. We'll worry about a destination once I get clear of the premises.

"Would you mind telling me what the HELL is going on?" I'm finally able to demand once we're safely under way.

"Just drive Anna, get us out of range. PLEASE."

"Where the hell am I supposed to go?"

He pauses to think. We're both visitors here, in truth, and we don't want to go back to Lacey's. This doesn't leave us with a lot of immediate options.

"Go back to moms."

I hate that place but I don't have a better suggestion to argue for. *Home, it is.* The problem with home is that it's not far enough away. Ten minutes down the road and we're already there, given the light traffic at this time of night. I back in to her driveway and kill the lights.

"Ok, can you tell me now what the hell is going on?"

"Everyone in our family is a freaking maniac!" Bobby sputters, looking genuinely in shock. "What the *hell* happened to everyone?!"

"Bobby, what the *hell* are you talking about? What happened while I was in the hospital?"

"Well, James and I were cold and dying of thirst after spending the better part of the evening locked in a metal box." This comment comes free with a dry look. "We decide to slip out to the convenience store across the street to grab a coffee while we wait."

"Ok... coffee. Yes, that's sinister."

"Anna! This is serious. It is very serious."

"Ok, ok, I'm sorry. Go on." I can refrain from sarcasm at least until I know who or what is in danger.

"Well, we're in there and James starts talking about Silver and how she's so heroic. She... she DID talk to us earlier. We lied. I was afraid to say anything, I didn't want to 'out' myself..."

"Out yourself?"

"Yeah, Silver started talking... About the family and how we could rise to terrible glory with a little organization. Pull together and be a merry little band of misfits. Lacey and James... they just ate it up. Well, actually, Lacey was eating it up and James was on board as soon as she showed interest. It came down to me. I was outclassed and didn't know what to do, so I pretended to go along with it."

Things are starting to fall in to place a little bit better but I still don't like where this is headed. This night gets more complicated with each passing hour.

"Ok, so you went along with it, then what?"

"Well... I think she knew. She could tell that I wasn't enthusiastic about it like the others, I think. She made us get in the trunk as a sign of faith. A *trust* exercise. She bound us too, telling us that if anyone found us then it would at least be a good alibi. I didn't want to do it but they made me. They made James too... the part he said about having a knife held on him was true. It was just for a different reason. To prove he wasn't scared. To prove he was worthy."

Half-truths. Half-lies. It's getting harder and harder to keep things straight, and I still don't have my knife back.

"So you got in the trunk. Did you know where she was going?" He shakes his head adamantly.

"No no, she didn't tell us that. She just said she wanted to go for a ride that way, based on the first part of the conversation. I can't believe I was stupid enough to play along." He starts to sniffle.

"Shh, shh, it's okay. Keep going, what happened?"

"Aside from us getting stuck in the freezing car for a couple hours?" I nod, hoping he'll continue. "Once we got here, to the hospital, James tells me what a visionary Silver is, and how great teaming up would be.

Then he just starts going on and on about Lacey, and keeping her safe and watching over her without having to hide... I... I just don't know what the hell is going on any more, Anna. What the hell happened to us?" He's bordering on tears again. I just let him go. Often times the worst thing to do is to tell someone not to cry, it's almost like pulling a teardrop trigger.

"Bobby... Do you trust me?" He rubs his eyes hard, trying to fight the swelling lump in his throat. I get half a nod. I'll have to take it. "Bobby, everything I said to you so far has been true. Silver is the one to blame for this mess here. She went psycho and has it in for me. Apparently she has for years..." I can't fight the wistful sigh. Bobby doesn't miss a beat.

"What does that mean for us?"

"It means - she has a habit of setting me up for unfortunate situations. Let's just leave it at that. As it stands right now she's trying to pin the whole night, and anything else that's come up, on me. I have to get the fuck out of this town."

"No, Anna, don't leave me!" He almost shrieks. I put my hands up in the air to make him stop. Thankfully it works.

"Wait... wait, Bobby, wait." I have to talk between his sniffles. "First, I have a very *very* important question for you. This is VERY important, and I will be able to tell if you're lying to me, okay? I need to know the answer for this before I know if I can help you or not, okay? I won't judge you either way, but I need to know." I feel like I'm talking down a jumper from a ledge.

He nods and tries to get himself under better control. The tears stop streaming but the remnant of sobs are still heavy on his breath. He draws in a few full lungs of air and nods his head. He's ready.

"Bobby, this is very important... Have you ever killed anybody?"

Bobby looks stricken, perhaps even a bit aghast.

"What? Why would you even ask that?"

"It's important. Answer the question, please." *Keep the voice steady. Don't spook the kid.*

"How could you even think something like that?" He looks truly perplexed, but he's stalling. He can't tell which answer I'm waiting to hear from him.

"Bobby." Serious tone, solemn look.

"Oh for fuck's sake! No, Anna, I've never killed anyone. Why?"

"I just needed to know. And I'd like to keep it that way. Maybe there is a little hope." He looks so confused, and I can't really blame him. If he's telling the truth, he's really the only one who has his hands clean, other than Stephen. Maybe we're not all bad. Dysfunctional sure, but show me any family who can't lay some claim to that birthright.

Mother's house looks empty and hollow already. No sign of life, no light, no soul. You can tell when you pass by a vacant house. There's always something about them that looks a little forlorn, a little neglected, even if it's only been a day, or a week, or a month. The energy of the inhabitants not coursing through its wires and wood has a telling effect. Her house is already dead, severed from human contact. Already the haunting begins. The curious noises, the unfamiliar creaks. Enough to put passers-by ill at ease and hurry their step when walking past the threshold of loneliness.

"Anna?" My trance is broken but my voice is hushed.

"Yes, Bobby?"

"We need to go inside." I nod but I don't understand why.

It feels unnatural standing outside of her door. Voices from arguments past echo in my ears, and I wince in reflex as an imaginary vase hurtles towards my head.

Flashbacks aren't just for veterans... although I guess I am a veteran of my own wars at that.

Bobby tips over a garden gnome nestled in the overgrown shrubs adjacent to the steps and reveals a spare key. The gnome has been there as long as I can remember, the faded paint chipped and the edges tattered and worn. As a child I rescued it from a neighborhood garage sale. I couldn't believe someone would cast off such a colorful and delightful creature for only a nickel. It was my first in a collection of ceramic fey folk. At one point in time I had a fairly circle closely guarding a mound of daffodils. It was glorious.

Only the gnome remained. Children running rough shod, angry fathers, and lawn equipment cut most of them down in their upcycled prime. Neighborhood teenagers took care of the rest. I guess there was something about being the first, establishing a presence, that kept him here all of these years; an icon of a happier time. It was a shame his glory and splendor was gone from summers of parched heat and winters of salt and snow. Everything has its season. Everything has its time. Everything passes by the wayside eventually, and returns to the earth only to be forgotten.

The hinges give a disgruntled creak as if the door has been sealed tight for millennia. It's only been a week, give or take, since someone has been through this threshold. The spirit is indeed gone. Surprisingly, the entry is still quite cozy and warm, betraying the contrast of the uninviting sight from the exterior. No one's been by to take care of the utilities yet, or even looked at the estate so there is still work to be done. Everything is as it was left when mother was rushed to the hospital; even her tea cup sits on the table, half empty and showing a shimmering rainbow on the surface of the liquid that should otherwise be molding. I leave it be -- no doubt this was the final dose that put her over the top. Someone else can take care of her poison.

It's hard not to survey the room. The time that has passed since I've been in this very spot is evident in the furnishings and the finishes that have been updated over the years. In truth, other than the bones of the place, there's not much that I really find that familiar. Sure, the rooms are in the same configuration, even the woodwork is in the same place but colors and carpets and wall coverings have updated themselves without any hint of my existence. And that's okay by me. It's actually easier to look around and not have the sentimental attachment. This is a different place; much of the terror and pain has been patched and painted and plastered over. In a strange way I'm glad to see there was progress, yet it makes me feel somewhat invalidated based on my experiences. All the pain could be washed away with a fresh coat of paint and some new gingham curtains.

A few little molds of hand prints and footprints and pictures of thanksgiving turkeys made out of hands still grace the walls in a macabre museum of our past. There's nothing left of mine, I have been erased. Silver and Stephen seem to have suffered a similar fate, though there are a few small tokens of their youth collecting dust in the far corners. Leaving meant severances from the family tree. If only it were that easy. If only the damaged limb didn't tingle and twitch once it was amputated.

Bobby looks intent. He's searching for something in the house; I can't imagine what could possibly be so important to come back for.

"Bobby, we should just go. Let's get out of here. I can take you to the closest airport and you can go back home and be safe. You have a wife to think about, you know..."

"I know." Is all he says but the look on his face stays focused just the same. *Sigh.*

"What is so god damned important? What are you looking for?" My eyes keep casting to the windows, watching the driveway. I half expect a family reunion of peasants with torches to come crashing through the door. I don't like it here. I feel exposed and I don't like it at all.

Bobby starts flinging open drawers and cupboards, prying through everything, looking in old coffee cans and over-sized cookie jars.

"If I know what you're looking for, I can help you try to find it." Anything to get us out of here quicker. He ignores me. He's on a mission.

Wandering through the house, I try to speculate what he could possibly be in search of. Money? Jewelry? Unlikely. He doesn't seem like the type that would be concerned with carrying around a hefty bank roll at the expense of being lynched by his siblings.

Tearing through the living room and dining room proves futile. He moves on to the kitchen. Systematically he goes through the same search process, again turning up empty handed. The glistening sweat on his brow adds to the frustrated look growing on his face. Slumped shoulders and a hanging head, flop back against the old refrigerator sitting in the corner; a look of defeat is on his face.

"Bobby, talk to me. What's wrong? What are you looking for?"

"Maybe I was wrong... I thought it would be here..." He only talks to himself.

"What are you looking for? Did you check the bedrooms? How about upstairs?" He just shakes his head.

"No, no, I know it's here... That's too careless, too casual, she wouldn't leave it there..."

"Bobby, wouldn't leave *what?*" He hits his head off of the freezer door again, bouncing it like he's trying to jog his memory physically.

"She would put it someplace safe, someplace unexpected but someplace that could be easily..." He stops dead in his tracks, a light glowing in his eyes. Immediately he spins around, face to face with the freezer door. "...found in case of emergency!" The freezer door flies open and he pries an iced up coffee can out of the permafrost. He doesn't even open it to know if he's found the object of his quest - a light shake says it all.

Bobby runs to the table and flips off the lid, spilling the frosted contents on to the plastic table cloth. Piles of newspaper clippings and small handwritten notes tumble out of it, but the big thunk is what grabs my attention. A flash of bluing peeks through the yellow and white papers.

He starts flipping through the news clippings and notes. From a distance I can see the headings on each one. Most of them say "James" or "Silver," some say "Lacey" and a small pile clipped together says "Anna." Only a couple say "Stephen" and none appear to say "Bobby." He hastily sorts out the piles per names as quick as he can. As he gets through the rats nest, the true objective comes to view. The Colt Lawman - snub nose .357, a fully loaded six shooter.

My feet take me closer to the table despite my brain being unconvinced that this is the appropriate response. Bobby pulls the pistol aside from the pile, away from me and near to him. As of yet he doesn't appear to be focused on the equalizer. A hesitant finger reaches out and draws over a small stack of clippings. I flip through them, looking at the hand scrawled notes on the tops. Names, dates, locations... it's all there. Or at least almost all there.

-31-

She's tracked us, all these years. All this time she knew, or at least suspected, what her children were capable of. The ones with Stephen's name talked mainly of fires. The ones labeled Silver appeared to have performance reviews stapled to the local police blotter reports of foul play and married men showing up dead and robbed at cheap hotels. Lacey's snippets read like a list of nursing home exposés with notes of mysterious deaths and no suspects. Hand written notes seemed to fill in the gaps. Suspicions, ideas and pieces she had to put together herself that the media overlooked.

It is one hell of a family scrapbook.

My knees betray me, giving out. I collapse in a chair, head spinning. I had no idea the depth of scope and amount of ground that we had covered over the years; it was truly devastating. Most of the notes with "James" listed were of the handwritten variety. It looked like a 'who's who' of Lacey's suitors and romantic entanglements over the years, and their equally uncanny disappearances. There is even a proposed theory about the rose garden outside Lacey's window where she was first set to run away with her Romeo. Apparently the roses bloom best there and according to the accounts, she dared not dig too deep.

I prop up my head as I watch Bobby continue to sort the piles out and fasten them together with stray displaced paper clips from the can. One by one he puts our resumes together, offering up no explanation. My eyes stick on the gun, waiting to face the wrong end of the action.

Patiently, I wait. Just looking. Just watching. At the last handwritten note Bobby pauses, a flicker of grief in his eyes. He hands it to me.

I don't know how this came to pass. How I could be the bearer of such a burdensome brood. I didn't mean for it to end this way, of that I'm sure. Given the chance, I will right my wrongs and make peace for the sins of their father. Giving my children the sweet rest they deserve is the only way. I hope then, I've finally been enough. Forgive me.

Bobby picks up the gun and flips open the chamber in a natural movement. I crane my neck to share his view. My blood runs cold when I realize the bullets are labeled... and there's one for me.

"Bobby?" He frowns, but not in my direction.

"We should get out of here. We need to get out of here." Mild natured, free loving Bobby Ray has suddenly taken on a commanding air that I've never really seen, and right now I'm not going to argue. "I just wanted the information... I knew she kept it here somewhere, I found it before. Damn kids and their curiosity..." The small smile on his face is not reflected in his eyes. For once he looks cold, disappointed.

Lady luck is not going to favor me twice in one night. Two steps towards the door and I see headlights flicker on the houses next to us. Everything else is quiet. I know that vehicle is coming for me, for us. I grab Bobby's arm, but he's already seen them too.

"Shit!" He spits through his teeth. He slips the gun into the back of his pants and shoves the papers back into the can.

"Can we go out the back? I don't know if we can get to the car but we'll at least have a chance to scatter on foot." Bobby shakes his head vehemently.

"It won't work. Mom kept it locked up tight the past few years, problems with the neighborhood. Once she was living here all alone she got extra paranoid. The only way out is up and over the fence and by the time we do that we'll be sitting ducks. We're fucked."

They waste no time with proper parking. The pick-up truck chirps its tires as it comes to a halt in front of my car, blocking it in. *Double shit.* Dim street lights reveal the flickers of bodies in motion as they pour out of the cab like a swarm of flying monkeys. I see the cowboy hat. It's not on my side.

Alan needlessly sends a foot through the door jamb, Marshall-style, with Silver and Lacey hot on his heels. I grab for my knife. My knife which I no longer have. *Fuck. Me.*

The look down the barrel of a .45 isn't quite how I pictured it, but the deliberate time he takes to rack the action is what sends my stomach to the floor. Bobby and I are frozen, trapped, cornered like rats. This is most disappointing. Silver is barking orders to the dynamic duo that I can't seem to decipher in the chaos. Alan's gray eyes are staring me down over the iron sites, his jaw set. *What a waste.*

"So Alan, is this how it ends? You're just another flunky henchman?" His eyes burn a hole through me. "Weren't you sworn to uphold the law, or was that all part of the show?" His jaw twitches, I can see his resolve wavering.

"It's not like that... I didn't want this..." is all he whispers.

"Are you sure? Because that certainly seems to be what's unfolding here. I thought you were better than that. I thought you were noble." I'm going for broke, maybe I can talk him down, maybe I can't, but it's my only hope at the moment and it buys me time.

His head dips slightly, for a moment he takes his

eyes away, unable to look at me. The gun doesn't waver.

"Would you just shoot her?! What the hell are you waiting for?!" Silver is eager for blood, stomping her foot like the petulant child she is. She wants it and she wants it now. Alan affords her a sidelong glance but keeps my body in his range. He has no words of wisdom, no witty retort, his jaw just pulsates with the muscles grinding his teeth together. "If you don't fucking shoot her, I will!" Silver grabs for the gun but Alan resists.

Lacey screams as my ringing ears cry for attention and my left shoulder burns with molten lead. I hit the floor like a ton of bricks, writhing on the red Persian rug.

"You son of a bitch! You fucking turncoat coward!" The spittle froths at the corners of my mouth as I cry out in pain induced rage. I swear I hear Silver laugh.

Another two cracks and a scream. A cowboy shaped pile of crap now lays on the floor. I look up long enough to see Bobby holding the butt of a now smoking .357, his face ashen as paper. Silver and Lacey stare at him, stunned.

"Bobby..." Is all I can manage before I see him crumple and fall to the floor, crimson traces pouring through his shirt from his abdomen. There is no writhing from him, he's still.

I stare at Silver through a haze of hot tears and bloody hands. She's never looked more joyous, even with the stitches and black eye I afforded her earlier in the evening. Torture becomes her. She was born and bred to do this and it shows.

A soft moan escapes Bobby's lips as his fingers twitch, just enough to catch Silver's attention.

"Lacey, go get that gun for me, will you dear? And be careful, wouldn't want to have any accidents now, would we? I need to have a little chit chat with Anna." Cruelness paints her lips red. Silver leans over and plucks Alan's gun from his cooling, dying hand. Lacey stands, still frozen in her tracks, staring at Bobby as the crimson pool flows under him.

"Did I already miss all the fun?" I hear James' voice boost from the back kitchen door behind us. Bastard must have scaled the fence and came in as backup. We were outflanked and had no idea. They were ready for slaughter.

"LACEY, the GUN." Silver snipes, strutting across the room to meet me with a kick, her bells jingling merrily. I've seen enough of these boots for one day. "LACEY!" She bellows with a stomp.

Finally snapped out of her trance, Lacey scurries across the room towards Bobby. A faint twitch, I see it. She doesn't. A careless reach and another sharp crack. Bobby lays a final shot between Lacey's eyes at point blank range. The look on her face shows shock and surprise as she hits the floor, a pile of blood, brain and blond ringlets circling her head like a horrid halo. My stomach lurches and I try not to vomit. At least good fortune grants me that much.

A bellow of distraught rage echoes from the kitchen the moment she comes to rest on the floor. James tears in to the room, bounding towards Lacey with lightning speed, stopping short at Bobby. In one neat move, he has Bobby on his feet, suspended by his collar. The gun still flops loosely in Bobby's hand as his head lolls around in a state of semi-conscious shock, side soaked in blood from resting in the pools of his own life force.

"What the HELL did you do? Why? Why would you do that? She wouldn't have done anything to you! How could you hurt her?!" He shakes Bobby like a rag doll. The motion is enough to bring him back to fleeting lucidity.

Bobby struggles to get free of James but his strength is clearly fading. In any other circumstance, seeing the two grapple would just be a regular brotherly fight, but not today. Bobby snuffed the life out of his beloved right before his eyes. There would be no shaking hands and making nice. Not tonight.

James wrenches on his wrist, trying to pull the gun out of his still vice like grip. Bobby manages to fight him off as I struggle to get to my feet. One knee is up off the ground when I feel the sensation of a sharp blade crushing near the middle of my spine. The stunning blow from Silver sends me sprawling on to my shoulder and screaming in pain once again. The clatter and chime from her hemlines mock me. Her garter dagger sticks behind my shoulder blade, making it difficult to roll away from her.

"Bloody hell!" Silver spits and raises her new gun to take aim at the fighting dogs. Neither James nor Bobby realizes they're now in the cross hairs as the two intertwine in struggle. Silver stands, waiting for a clear shot at Bobby, grinding her heel into the back of my calf as she waits. No amount of rolling or whimpering seems to get me out from under her stilettos, but it will gain me a blade.

James releases Bobby, trying to gain space to maneuver. Silver picks her shot as I roll, which sends her off balance from trying to drive her heel through my leg. Another muzzle flash, another collapse. She has missed and she has missed bad; this is what you get for being cocky. Lacey now has James to watch over her for eternity.

"MOTHER FUCKER!" She jabs me with her heel again and makes me scream. Bobby is back down, each breath growing shallower as the oozing blood turns dark and thick. Silver storms over to him like a witch in flight. "WHAT." Kick. "THE HELL." Kick. "Did you MAKE..." Kick. "Me DO!" Kick again. He barely can muster a whimper of pain.

"You little piece of shit," she growls through her teeth at him. "You just couldn't mind your own business." She checks her gun and cues up the next round, unaware that my legs are indeed working, despite her best efforts. She starts to grind her heel on him too, going for a little more torture before she ends his valiant efforts, like any good psychotic villain. Overconfidence, however, is often what leads to their great demise.

"You destroyed my tribe, my band of merry misfits. What you don't realize is that you too, are already dead..." Her gun rises in line with Bobby's face, his fluttering eyelids the only response on his ashen, clammy face. She slowly draws the bead down for effect. "Kiss my a--..."

"Leave him alone you *fucking* bitch." A hand full of hair and a sharp tug throws her off balance and snaps her neck backwards into my chest. Despite the searing pain in my shoulder I hold her tight. I don't give her the time to finish the witty repartee; her knife hits her smooth and fast, hardly any resistance slipping through her skin and into cartilage. A gurgle, a gasp, and I throw her to the floor like the piece of trash she was.

"Bobby... no..." I collapse beside him, the waves of shock rolling over me. His shallow breath runs ragged, lungs filling with blood. I reach out to stroke his face, but his skin is too cold to touch. He's at the point of no return.

"Did... I... do good?" He struggles to get each word out without suffocating on blood. "Is... it... finally... done?"

"Yes, Bobby it's done. It's finally done." A faint smile traces his lips as the stillness takes him. "Be at peace, my brother."

I cry.

-32-

The road unfolds in front of me, dashed lines whizzing by in a familiar pattern, glowing circles of street lights flickering a steady rhythm. My tired eyes keep straying to the coffee can and garden gnome buckled in, riding shotgun. The depth of our disgrace lies beside me, a macabre scrapbook of the family history. A history I'd rather not be party to. But I can't forget. I shouldn't forget.

Shifting in my seat makes me wince; every part of me hurts in a unique way. It's difficult to take care of back wounds on your own, even more so with an injured wing. Mother still had enough medical supplies on hand from the old days that I was able to perform some reasonable emergency self-triage. I wish I had the luxury of time to take a shower but the amount of gunshots and screams that rang out in the night will not go unheeded for long.

A bottle of iodine, a few stitches where the bullet entered, some butterflies for the miscellaneous cuts and stab wounds, a pack of gauze for the exit wound and a fresh change of clothes pulled from her drawer makes me feel like a bedraggled but refreshed woman before I leave the house burning behind me. I take no chances in leaving anything behind. This monument to pain is no longer welcome to taint the night air. No other families should suffer its walls. The flames glow, glorious in red and orange, in my rear view mirror. Stephen would be proud.

The local press and law enforcement will have a field day reconstructing the scene. It will be the talk of the town for another twenty years, if not longer. The day the "Shaw House" triggered by the death of their ailing matriarch, went berserk would go down in the dark history of stories only whispered at late night sleepovers and Halloween bonfires. Families will murmur and talk about the children they knew growing up and going through school, reminiscing about our erratic behavior, strange clothes, constant bruises, and battle scars and general weirdness. Only then would they put it together. The years of abuse, the number of people who let it slip through their hands because they didn't want to cause a scene... it all came together.

The elder generation would dismiss it all, claiming abuse was just old school correction and that was just how it was back then. It was what they did; it was what everyone did. And that would make it all okay... because if one was guilty, then all were guilty.

The news about Clark would come out, no doubt tied in to the evil plans of the murderous family. I could hope for that at least, that the focus not be solely set on me. The rapist from the bar could be included in the party. Perhaps any interest in me would die with Silver as they took dental records and bone scans to determine who was really who in the end.

The community would mourn the loss of a law enforcement professional, clearly there to take the band down and make things right. He would get a hero's burial in the press, though the brass might know the real story. It would be easier to make him a martyr than a traitor no matter what the forensics may support. It spins better for public relations and cable news networks. The town would be turned on its head, a beacon of bad publicity, and it would profit off of our name on every corner for as long as it could.

Fresh money and a star in my pocket, thanks to Alan, will at least afford me a hot meal and a clean place to stay for the night off the grid. Besides, he won't be needing either item. After being such an ass, that's the least he can do for me. Right now all I want is put some distance between myself and that horrible human farm. This is why you should never go home again. My gut churns as a gentle reminder to heed its wisdom.

Some miles down the road and I can feel my weary body finally crashing on me. Time to pull off for the night; it's pointless to fight this far and wind up dead in a ditch. Maybe a hot meal and some rot-gut to ease the pain will suffice before I surrender this aching body to rest.

It's not long before a gas station and a small motel loom on the horizon. Antiquated neon lights flicker sporadically in the window behind the battered mini blinds, stained yellow from nicotine and grease. This will do nicely. My body screams protests about leaving the comfort of my driver's seat; a little extra effort is necessary to pull myself out without splitting a stitch. Only my stiff movement really discloses my condition - the few scuffs around my face are barely noticeable in the glow of the beer signs. I grit my teeth and head inside.

The locals don't bother to look up from their dollar drafts and stale bar popcorn. No seat at the end of the bar tonight - I couldn't be that fortunate. It's center stage for me, stuck right behind the beer taps. The only thing I can really see over them is the faded "restroom" sign. Not much of a view but at least I have my basic needs covered.

I crane my neck looking for drink options. The

collection of top shelf bottles, covered in dust and grime from years of neglect, reveals a pleasant surprise; a decent bourbon lurks above. Some aerobics and the wave of the adjacent drunk are involved to get the bartender to notice me over the taps, so I take advantage of his fleeting attention and order a double on the rocks. A war torn menu slides in front of me housed in a marinara stained plastic sleeve that was meant for a three ring binder. Fried basket of assorted fare it is; with a side of ranch of course, anything else would be 'uncivilized' and only draw attention. Sometimes when I sit in places like this I want to order escargot or caviar, just to see what they would do. This is not one of those nights.

The bourbon goes down hot and easy, just how I like it. Two tiny cubes pirouette in tandem as I swirl the glass absentmindedly, waiting for the food to arrive. The drink goes too quick. I need another. The beauty and terror of fried food is that it's fast and any flunky can run a fryer. Soon a piping hot basket of unidentifiable shapes slides in front of me. I take it on faith that all of the things presented to me are actually edible food products and not an assortment of inanimate objects dunked in batter for general amusement. For a fleeting moment I am content.

I gingerly gnaw on the first real food I've had in what seems like a week, trying not to sear every taste bud in my mouth as I mull over my situation. Disappearing should be a top priority, but that part is easy. I've done it more than once and I'm good at it. It will be especially easy without the anchor of Lacey trying to keep track of me as I bound from town to town. The only real connection I had is the one that nearly cost me my life.

The recent past is haunting me far more than the near future. If only the dead could speak I would know how this day got so damn out of hand. Guilty pangs fill me when I think of the innocents caught in our twisted little web. Bobby didn't deserve to die. He didn't deserve to sacrifice himself for me; I wasn't worth it. He was the one that should have gotten away, not me. Even *I* would have told him that if I would have had the chance. No doubt his wife would be devastated upon learning the news, her belief in the goodness of nature shaken to the core. I wish I could call her, tell her, but it wouldn't make it any better. Odds are she'd live her life hating me, wondering where I am and how I was so selfish as to take her loving husband away from her. She wouldn't understand. She couldn't.

My thoughts run to Alan. Had I missed a cue, a hint somewhere along the line? How did I even let him get that close to begin with? I should be better than that, a stronger judge of character. It isn't like me to let people slip under my radar so easily. The fact that I was weak worries me most. I don't like that I have to question my own judgment, question the one thing that has kept me safe time and time again.

How long ago had Silver actually be-spelled him? When he was watching her, following her, researching her movements and patterns? As he sat there in the night, doing surveillance, watching her trysts and erotic arts? Or maybe when he finally made contact with the elusive beast and he got the feel of her skin under his fingertips and the taste of her flesh on his lips. Perhaps her sweat was an opiate to the male sex. I wish I knew. What could she possibly offer him beyond carnal pleasures or brutal infamy? He surrendered it all for nothing, a life and a career thrown away on a disposable, despicable woman. Maybe the clippings would tell me more about her and her powers over men. Maybe they would just be cold facts and careful reports. The truth of the situation can stay in their ashen grave for all I care, it really doesn't matter now.

Another double. It doesn't burn quite the same this time; I'm numbing to the pain and my nerves thank me. The lonely drunks flanking me try occasional bursts of conversation but lack the presence of mind to stay on topic. It's easy to let the exchanges drop and go about my sipping. The tap system isn't a half bad place to be - no one jockeys to get in beside me because there's no worse spot at the bar. I'm going to have to remember this in the future. The bartender also doesn't get to flex his associate degree in Psychology on me this way. Win win.

The food settles in my stomach, causing a temporary fuzziness as the blood rushes from my extremities, eager to aid in digestion and to pump the alcohol to my tired brain. This can be the only explanation for my next leap in logic. *Stephen. I have to call Stephen.* He should hear it from me, not the nightly national news wire, and certainly not from a flurry of FBI agents staked out at his home.

Eyes unfocused on the "restroom" sign, I stare through the wall as I make a mental transcript of what I should say. How I should tell him, how much he should know, what I should do if he doesn't answer... I'm not coming up with any satisfying material. I notice a body hovering near the opening to the bathroom area. When it leaves, the glint of a pay-phone button catches my eye. Idly I finger the change from my check. Quarter on quarter, I tap as I deliberate. He has a right to know his entire family is gone, even if he doesn't care. Even I would want to have that information if only because it meant I no longer had to worry about people trying to dig me up for halfhearted family picnics, Christmas parties, or funerals.

The empty glass mocks me, waiting for a decision. I could drink enough to forget; that would be easy enough, but the last thing I need is added pain in the morning. My mind can be at rest for the first time if I get this out of my head and off my chest. The liquid courage kicks in and steels my resolve. Quarters at the ready, I work through the crowd towards the crusty old pay-phone, secretly hoping it's out of service. It's not.

Clink clink dial tone. I press in the number that I last remember for him. The line barely gets a ring completed before he picks up.

"Hello?"

"Stephen?" I'm not sure of my brother's voice.

"Yes. Who is this?"

"Stephen, it's Anna."

"Oh. Uh, hi." Awkward silence.

"Stephen, I need to talk to you."

"Is this about mom's estate? I told Lacey she could call me with questions." His tone is terse.

"No no, it's not about that. It's important though..." I can't find the words to spit out.

"...what is it? You sound upset actually. What's wrong, are you okay?"

"Yes, Stephen, I'm fine. Thank you." I pause. *Rip the band aid off. Just do it already.* "Actually, it's about the others..."

"The others? Why, what's going on?" Concern is building in his voice.

"Stephen... they're dead." Silence on the phone line. "Are... are you there?"

"What do you mean they're dead?" His voice sounds small with panic. "You can't mean *all* of them?" I sigh.

"Yes, all of them." My eyes are closed. I'm leaning against the phone cabinet like it's a dance partner. It's hard keeping my voice down low enough with the public milling around me.

"What the hell happened? Was there an accident?"

"No... not quite. Nothing like that. I... I don't really want to go in to details right now, but it's bad Stephen, it's real bad. We all turned on each other."

"Christ, Anna, what the hell are you talking about? All turned on each other? Are you saying they killed each other?" Disbelief echoes across the line.

"Basically, that's it. I'm sure you'll hear plenty about it on the news before too long. I imagine it's going to be quite the sensation..." My voice is still low and quiet.

I am not enjoying this.

"Are you fucking kidding me? You're serious about this?!" His voice is quiet and pinched now; things are starting to sink in. "How is this even possible? I still don't understand..."

"You can thank Silver for most of it. Turns out she had quite the checkered past from her traveling shows... and she convinced James and Lacey that the murdering vagabond lifestyle was the way to go..."

"Wait, what about Bobby? You didn't say anything about Bobby..." His concern is genuine.

"Bobby saved my life, Stephen. He sacrificed his life for mine, actually... and saved me from the others."

"Oh, Christ. *Christ, Anna*. I knew I should have come. I was supposed to but... I just didn't want to. I didn't want to be in that place again. I haven't been back in so long and things have been good, you know? I got out of the crazy and I didn't want to go back. But I should have been there... I should have come..."

"No, Stephen, no. It's best that you didn't. I don't think I could have handled losing all of my family in one day. It wouldn't have turned out any better, that I can almost say for sure. It was best that you stayed."

"But..."

"No. It was best you stayed, believe me." A twinge in my shoulder reminds me I need to change my bandages. A private room sounds really good right now.

"Oh, Anna... Oh I'm so sorry. I... I don't know if sorry is right? Is it? Should I be angry? Because what I'm feeling is some relief, and it's not right. It's not the right response to this... Logically, I know that. I'm not sure who to be sorry for and I don't want to seem cruel saying that I'm relieved. Does that make any sense?"

"Yes, Stephen, it does. More than you can imagine, trust me." I can see I'm gaining some attention from the bar patrons. I need to keep my damn voice down better. *Death* has a way of catching people's ears. "I just hope to God this thing doesn't bring dad out of the wood work. I don't think I could handle that. And I don't want any more blood on my hands..." My throat feels tight just from realizing the possibility.

Silence on the other end of the phone.

"Stephen?" The sudden silence has me concerned.

"I... I don't think that will be a problem, Anna, don't worry about it. Please." I hear the sigh on the other end of the line. It's like blood in the water. He knows something, I can taste it.

"Stephen... what do you mean?"

"I'd rather not..."

"*Stephen, please* tell me what you mean!"

"Our father won't be bothering anyone ever again. In fact, he hasn't been bothering anyone for a very long time." The insinuation makes my blood run cold.

"What are you saying?"

"What I'm saying is that none of our hands are clean, Anna." He pauses, collecting his thoughts. "After all of it. After all that abuse and shit he did to us, I saw him. I saw him walk into that house, all smiles and hugs. I watched them, night after night, after I found out. I couldn't let him live the lie any longer; it wasn't fair. They had everything. Everything we wanted and could never have, right down to a loving father..."

"Who, Stephen? Who the hell are you talking about?"

"Dad's second family."

-33-

The radio drones on. *Well I started out down a dirty road, started out all alone, and the sun went down as I crossed the hill, and the town lit up and the world go still...* Some things never change.

I sit in the car, back on the road. There will be no rest tonight. Nor tomorrow night. Nor the night after. The moment of peace I had is gone. Somewhere out there there are more of us. Somewhere along the streets and the subways they talk and breathe and breed. I can't sleep tonight. I can't sleep until the others rest. The cruelty of fate calls upon me to find them. The twisted. The sick. The broken.

ABOUT THE AUTHOR

Katherine Alton is a professional designer and an amateur herbalist who enjoys burying things in her garden. An avid fan of dystopian literature, she was drawn to the bittersweet and the macabre at an early age. Unable to shirk the unrelenting gray skies of the Great Lakes region, Katherine has been working on finding more constructive outlets for her creative impulses.

That don't involve digging.